U0022786

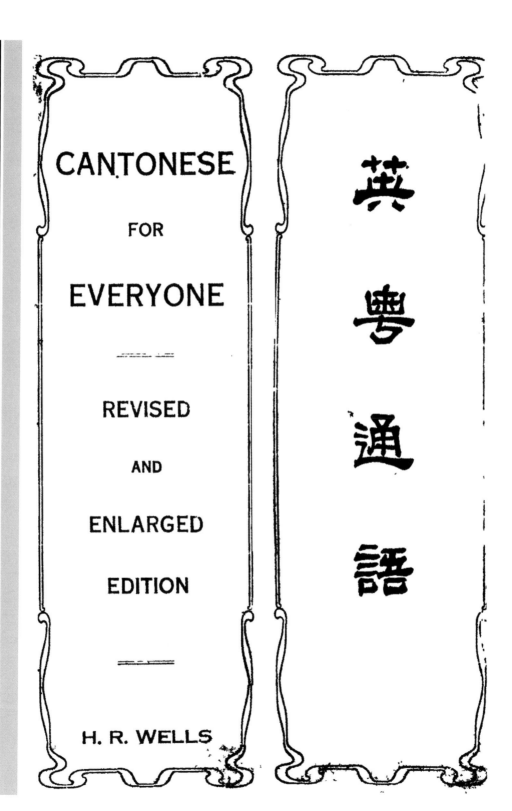

英粵通語 Cantonese for everyone ——香港大學粵語教材（一九三一）

CANTONESE

FOR

EVERYONE

——

REVISED

AND

ENLARGED

EDITION

——

H. R. WELLS

英粵通語

1

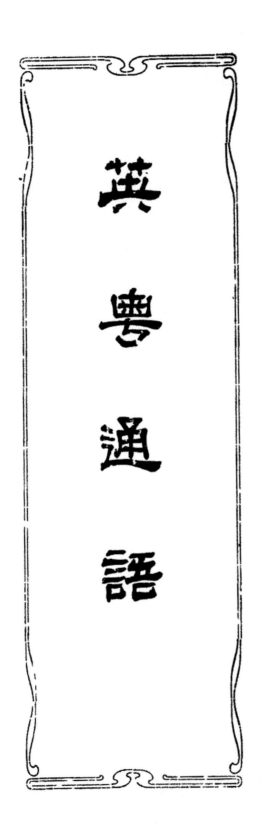

英粵通語

香港・澳門雙城成長經典

CANTONESE FOR EVERYONE

The Reverend H. R. WELLS, O.B.E.
London Mission,
Hong Kong.

———

Member of the Board of Examiners,
Hong Kong, for thirty years.
Director of Cantonese Class in
Hong Kong University for four years.

REVISED AND ENLARGED
EDITION

———

Printed by
KAE SHEAN PRINTING CO.,
59, Queen's Road Central
HONGKONG
1931.

INTRODUCTION.

This book is prepared to meet the needs of students wishing to get a fairly good command of Cantonese in a short time.

It must be learnt and used at the same time. Students should begin to talk from the start, a conversation is given after the first lesson, and may be used at once. Do not try to get a good vocabulary before beginning to speak.

It is better to employ a teacher, or join a class at first, but many can learn without this, if they really study, and practise the words.

When one has learnt the first ten lessons he has got material for constant use, and can go right forward. The first twenty lessons contain the key words to Cantonese, and sentences of all kinds are built on these words in the lessons and exercises.

The numbers will be found at the heads of the lessons, and lists of terminating words and classifiers, and a small extra vocabulary are printed on a separate sheet.

A table of tones or inflections is given, students should get some one to help them to understand these inflections.

Every word has its own inflection or tone, but some have also a changed tone, which is often indicated by an asterisk. A great many of the changed tones are rising inflections and are like the second high tone, a similar rising inflection is used in words of the fourth tone, which all end in k, p, or t, Paak₄ white is duplicated as *Paak₄ Paak₄, meaning " very white " and Paak₄ *Paak₄,—meaning " in vain."

The tones are in the natural pitch of one's voice, the high tones need not crack one's voice, nor the low tones become a growl.

It is necessary to get the correct inflection, as the wrong one means something else. Most people with practice and care can do quite well.

The tones are called First, second, third, and fourth high and low tones thus makes 8, and the middle fourth makes the ninth.

In Chinese the tones in the higher series, are called Sheung₃ P'ing₁ (even), sheung₃ sheung₃ (rising), Sheung₃ hui³ (departing) Sheung₃ yap₄ (entering) the lower series are Ha₃ p'ing₃, ha₃ sheung₃, ha₃ hui,³ and ha₃ yap₄, the middle one being chung¹ yap₄.

Tone marks are given by small figures 1, 2, 3, 4, at the upper right hand corner for higher tones, and the same figures at the lower right hand corner for lower tones; 0 being used for the middle fourth at the end of the word.

Take these sentences in English.

No₁ direct negative, No₁ first low tone.

Did you say no²? no² second high tone (element of surprise).

No₃ surely that cannot be so, No₃ third low tone. There is usually a slight holding on to the sound in this case. It is something like a note of a bell fading away.

You know quite well (strongly affirmative) Know¹ first high tone.

These are not absolute but are frequently used by us in this way.

The method of romanisation is that used in Canton in Romanised Bibles, and a primer of this may be obtained at the Bible store No. 2, Wyndham Street for 15 cts. The primer is not necessary, the sounds are clear, but do not always represent fully the sounds in Cantonese. The English alphabet does not contain certain sounds. Practise your sounds by ear and do not follow the romanised if it conveys the wrong sound to you.

In English we use a sound "er" in speaking.

Chinese use a number of finals such as a, che, ke, kwa, la, le, loh, lok, ma, me, moh, ne, ni, O, wa, and wo.

Some are phonetic, some emphatic, some euphonic, some interrogative, there are about 80 given in Mr. Dyer Ball's "Cantonese made Easy." Language experts may study these, but students will naturally get the usual ones as they learn, a short list is given to assist students, they are not included in the lessons, but some appear in the conversations.

Classifiers or numeratives are common in Chinese. nearly every noun has one, but there are only about 80 in all, a list of 20 is given, others will be learnt in practice. Some come in the lessons, see lessons 2₁; 4₅; 7₁; 8₅; 12₅; etc. They should be learnt by use, the average student cannot learn them all at once and use them correctly. Listen to others and adopt their classifiers. Absolute perfection in this matter is almost impossible in the case of non-Chinese students.

Sounds.— Cantonese sounds are changing, initial l is becoming n; and initial n, l. Variations are found in all districts.

Mistakes.— I fear students may find many mistakes, if they will try this type of proof reading they will see the difficulty.

"To err is human, to forgive divine. My humanity may be seen in the errata, let your forgiveness prove your divinity.

Do not be annoyed at the mistakes—correct them and smile.

April 1931.

CANTONESE COLLOQUIAL.

Table of Tone Exercise.

These should be practised frequently at first and occasionally afterwards.
When no character is given, no word of the sound given has been found.

	上平 sheung₁ p'ing₁ first high	上上 sheung₂ sheung₂ second high	上去 sheung₃ hui₃ third high	上入 sheung₄ yap₄ fourth high	中入 chung¹ yap₁ middle fourth	下平 ha₂ p'ing₁ first low	下上 ha₂ sheung₃ second low	下去 ha₃ hui₃ third low	下入 ha₄ yap₄ fourth low
High	⟶	/	/	⌐	⌐				
Low						⟶	/	/	⌐
1	因 yan^1	忍 yan^2	印 yan^3	一 yat^4	○	人 yan_1	引 yan_2	刃 yan_3	日 yat_4
2	邊 pin^1	貶 pin^2	變 pin^3	必 pit^1	鱉 pit_0	○ pin_1	○ pin_2	便 pin_3	別 pit_4
3	衣 i^1	椅 i^2	意 i^3	○	○	而 i_1	耳 i_2	二 i_3	○
4	央 $yeung^1$	鞅 $yeung^2$	怏 $yeung^3$	約 $yeuk^1$	約 $yeuk_0$	羊 $yeung_1$	仰 $yeung_2$	樣 $yeung_3$	若 $yeuk_4$
5	謙 him^1	險 him^2	欠 him^3	○ hip^1	怯 hip_0	○ him_1	○ him_2	○ him_3	挾 hip_4

I am indebted to Mr. Sung Hok Pang for permission to use this table which was used somewhat in this form by him.

英粵通語 Cantonese for everyone —— 香港大學粵語教材（一九三一）

CONTENTS

CONTENTS—(*Continued*).

英粵通語 Cantonese for everyone ——香港大學粵語教材 (一九三一)

THE FIRST LESSON

第 一 課—Tai. yat⁴ foh⁹

1	我	Ngoh₂ (ngaw₂)—*I*	6	有	Yau₂—*Have, is, yes*
2	行	Haang₁—*Walk, go*	7	冇	Mo₂—*Not, no, have not*
3	你	Nei₂ (nay₂)—*You*	8	唔	M₁—*Not, negative*
4	見	Kin⁹ (geen³)—*See, feel*	9	係	Hai₃—*Is, was, to be, Yes*
5	人	Yan₁—*Man, person some one*	10	來, 嚟	Loi₁ lai₁—*To come*

1 我 Ngoh₂

2 我行 Ngoh₂ haang₁

3 你行 Nei₂ haang₁

4 我見你行 Ngoh₂ kin nei₂ haang₁

5 你見人行 Nei₂ kin⁹ yan₁ haang₁

6 有人見我行 Yau₂ yan₁ kin⁹ ngoh₂ haang₁

7 有人行冇 ? Yau₂ yan₁ haang₁ mo₂ ?

8 我唔見有人行 Ngoh₂ m₁ kin⁹ yau₂ yan₁ haang₁.

9 你係唔係見人行 ? Nei₂ †hai₃ m₁ hai₃ kin⁹ yan₁ haang₁?

10 有人嚟冇 ? Yau₂ yan₁ lai₁ mo₂ ?

1 I.

2 I am walking, or, I walk.

3 You walk

4 I saw you walking.

5 You saw a man walking.

6 There was a man (who) saw me walking.

7 Is there a man walking ?

8 I have not seen a man walking.

9 Did you see a man walking ?

10 Has a man come ?

Two sounds to this word

Another spelling is attached to some words as a guide to those who used my first method, which I think is the easiest method of spelling for English people.

† Hai₃ m₁ hai₃. This is a common idiom in Chinese; is, not is? i.e. yes or no ?

The First Exercise—(Conversation.)

1 Did you see a man come ?
   Nei₂ yau₂ kin³ yan₁ lai₁ mo₂ ?
   你 有 見 人 嚟 冇?

2 Yes, I saw a man come.
   Yau₂, ngoh₂ kin³ yau₂ yan₁ lai₁.
   有, 我 見 有 人 嚟.

3 Did you see me come ?
   Hai₃ kin³ ngoh₂ lai₁ m₁ hai₃ ?
   係 見 我 嚟 唔 係?

4 No, I saw a person come.
   M₁ hai₂, ngoh₂ kin³ yan₁ lai₁.
   唔 係, 我 見 人 嚟.

5 Did a person see you ?
   Yau₂ yan₁ kin¹ nei₂ mo₂ ?
   有 人 見 你 冇?

6 Yes, a person saw me.
   Yau₂, yau₂ yan₁ kin³ ngoh₂.
   有, 有 人 見 我.

7 Is anyone walking ?
   Yau₂ yan₁ haang₁ mo₂ ?
   有 人 行 冇?

8 No, no-one is walking.
   Mo₂, mo₂ yan₁ haang₁.
   冇, 冇 人 行.

9 Will you come (or not) ?
   Nei₂ lai₁ m₁ lai₁ ?
   你 嚟 唔 嚟.

10 I will come.
   Ngoh₂ lai₁. 我 嚟.

11 Did you come to see me ?
   Nei₂ lai₁ kin³ ngoh₂ hai₃ m₁ hai₃ ?
   你 嚟 見 我 係 唔 係.

12 Yes, I came to see you.
   Hai₃, ngoh₂ lai₁ kin³ nei₂
   係, 我 嚟 見 你.

THE SECOND LESSON

第 二 課—Tai₃ i₂ foh³

1	个	Koh⁵—*One, a piece, a numerative, or classifier* Koh² *that*	**6** 佢	K'ui₂—*He, him, she, it*
2	兩	Leung₂—*Two, a couple*	**7** 男	Naam₁—*Man, male.*
3	乜	Mat⁴—*What, who, why*	**8** 女	Nui₂—*Woman, female, girl*
4	野	Ye₂—*Thing*	**9** 呢	Ni¹ (nee)—*This, (at end of sentence, a question)*
5	做	Tso₃—*To make, be, do*	**10** 啲	Ti¹ (tik⁴) — *This, some, with ni¹ and koh³ often plural.*

---

1 有一个人見你行冇? Yau₂ yat⁴ koh³ yan₁ kin³ nei₂ haang₁ mo₂ ?

1 Did a man see you walking?

2 有, 有兩个人見我. Yau₂, yau₂ leung₂ koh⁵ yan₁ kin³ ngoh₂.

2 Yes, two people saw me.

3 乜人嚟. Mat⁴ yan₁ lai₁ ?

3 Who (what man) has come?

4 你兒乜野人嚟. Nei₂ kin⁵ mat⁴ ye₂ yan₁ lai₁?

4 What man did you see coming?

5 我兒人做野. Ngoh₂ kin² yan₁ tso₃ ye₂.

5 I saw a man working (doing something).

6 佢係乜野人呢. K'ui₂ hai₃ mat⁴ ye₂ yan₁ ni¹ ?

6 What kind of person was be?

7 佢係男人 K'ui₂ hai₃ naam₁ *yan₁.

7 He was a man.

8 係女人唔係呢. Hai₃ nui₂ *yan₁ m₁ hai₃ ni¹ ?

8 Was she a woman?

9 呢个係男人. Ni¹ koh³ hai₃ naam₁ *yan₁.

9 This is a man.

10 呢啲係女人. Ni¹ ti¹ hai₃ nui₂ *yan₁.

10 These are women.

†Yare² (without an r sound).

The Second Exercise—(Conversation.)

1 What is that man doing?
Koh² koh³ yan₁ tso₃ mat⁴ ye₂?
个 个 人 做 乜 野

2 He has come to see you.
K'ui₂ lai₁ kin⁵ nei₂.
佢 嚟 見 你

3 Has this man any work to do?
Ni¹ koh³ yan₁ yau₂ ye₂ tso₃ mo₂?
呢 个 人 有 野 做 冇

4 That man has no work.
Koh² koh⁵ yan₁ mo₂ ve₂ tso₃.
个 个 人 冇 野 做.

5 Has a woman come?
Yau₂ nui₂ *yan₁ lai₁ mo₂?
有 女 人 嚟 冇

6 No, no woman has come.
Mo₂, mo₂ nui₂ yan₁ lai₁.
冇, 冇 女 人 嚟

7 Has he come to see you?
K'ui₂ hai₃ lai₁ kin⁵ nei₂ m₁ hai₃?
佢 係 嚟 見 你 唔 係.

8 No, he came to see those two men.
M₁ hai₃, k'ui₂ lai₁ kin⁵ koh² leung₂ koh⁵ yan₁.
唔 係, 佢 嚟 見 个 兩 个 人

9 Why did you not come?
T'so₃ mat⁴ nei₂ m₁ lai₁?
做 乜 你 唔 嚟

10 I had work to do.
Ngoh₂ yau₂ ye₂ tso₃.
我 有 野 做.

THE THIRD LESSON

第 三 課—Tai₃ saam¹ foh³

1	好	Ho²—*Good, very.*	6	買	Maai₂—*Buy.*
2	幾	Kei²—*Several, how, fairly.*	7	少	Shiu²— *Few, small quantity.*
3	多	Toh¹—*Many.*	8	得	Tak⁴—*Get, can, able.*
4	要	Iu³—*Want, must, wish*	9	去	Hui³—*Go, away.*
5	銀	Ngan₁—*Silver, money.*	10	講	Kong²—*To talk, speak*

1 呢啲野好唔好. Ni¹ ti' ye₂ ho² m₁ ho²?

2 个啲幾好. Koh² ti' kei² ho².

3 幾多个人嚟. Kei² toh¹ koh¹ yan₁ lai₁?

4 你要乜野. Nei₂ iu⁵ mat⁴ ye₂?

5 我要啲銀. Ngoh₂ iu³ ti¹ ngan₁.

6 佢買野. K'ui₂ maai₂ ye₂.

7 我有好少銀. Ngoh₂ yau₂ ho² shiu² ngan₁.

8 好多銀買得好少野. Ho² toh¹ ngan₁ maai₂ tak⁴ ho² shiu² ye₂.

9 我要去. Ngoh₂ iu¹ hui³.

10 唔好講人. M₁ ho² kong² yan₁.

1 Are these things good or not?

2 Those are very good.

3 How many people are coming?

4 What do you want?

5 I want money.

6 He is buying things.

7 I have very little money.

8 A lot of money will buy very few things

9 I must go.

10 Do not talk about people.

* Hui was spelt Hou in the former book. This sound must be carefully practised.

The Third Exercise—(Conversation.)

1 What is this ?

Ni¹ ti¹ hai₃ mat⁴ ye₂ ?

呢 的 係 乜 野

2 That is money.

Koh² ti¹ hai₃ ngan₁.

个 的 係 銀

3 How much money have you ?

Nei₂ yau₂ kei² toh¹ *ngan₁ ?

你 有 幾 多 銀.

4 I have not much money.

Ngoh₂ mo₂ kei² toh¹ ngan₁.

我 冇 幾 多 銀.

5 Is he talking about me ?

K'ui₂ hai₃ kong² ngoh₂ m₁ hai₃ ?

佢 係 講 我 唔 係

6 He is not talking about you, but about going to buy things.

M₁ hai₃ kong² nei₂, kong² hui³ maai₂ ye₂.

唔 係 講 你, 講 去 買 野.

7 Could you arrange not to go ?

Nei₂ m₁ hui³ tak⁴ m₁ tak⁴ ni¹ ?

你 唔 去 得 唔 得 呢

8 I cannot (not go).   I must go.

Ngoh₂ m₁ hui⁵ m₁ tak⁴.

我 唔 去 唔 得

9 Is this good money (silver) ?

Ni¹ koh³ hai₅ ho² *ngan₁ m₁ hai₃ ?

呢 个 係 好 銀 唔 係.

10 That money is not very good.

Koh² koh³ *ngan₁ m₁ hai₃ kei² ho².

个 个 銀 唔 係 幾 好

11 Can I buy things with this money ?

Ni¹ ti¹ *ngan₁ maai₂ tak⁴ ye₂ m₁ ni¹ ?

呢 啲 銀 買 得 野 唔 呢

12 It will buy things, the money is good money.

Maai, tak⁴, ti¹ *ngan₁ hai₃ ho² *ngan₁.

買 得, 的 銀 係 好 銀

香港・澳門雙城成長經典

THE FOURTH LESSON

第 四 課—Tai₂ sz⁵ foh⁵

1	知	Chi²—*Know.*
2	識	Shik⁴— *Know, knowledge.*
3	咁	*Kom³—*So, such.*
4	樣	*Yeung₃—*Style, way, method.*
5	點	Tim²—*Why, a dot, an hour.*
6	聽	T'eng¹— *To hear, listen.*
7	解	Kaai²—*Explain.*
8	街	Kaai¹—*A street.*
9	條	T'iu₁—*A length, classifier for long things*
10	路	Lo₃—*A road, a way.*

1 我知你嚟. Ngoh₂ chi¹ nei₂ lai₁.

2 佢唔識你. K'ui₂ m₁ shik⁴ nei₂.

3 呢啲野冇个啲野咁好. Ni¹ ti¹ ye₂ mo₂ koh² ti¹ ye₂ kom³ ho² ?

4 你要幾多樣野呢. Nei₂ iu³ kei² toh¹ yeung₅ ye₂ ni¹ ?

5 點做好呢. Tim² tso₃ ho² ni¹ ?

6 好多人聽佢講. Ho² toh¹ yan₁ t'eng¹ k'ui₂ kong².

7 解我聽得唔得呢. Kaai² ngoh₂ t'eng¹ tak⁴ m₁ tak⁴ ni¹ ?

8 我去行街. Ngoh₂ hui³ haang₁ kaai¹.

9 个條係街. Koh² t'iu₁ hai₂ kaai¹.

10 行路去. Haang₁ lo₃ hui³.

1 I knew you were coming.

2 He does not know you.

3 These things are not as good as those.

4 How many kinds of things do you want ?

5 What is the best way to do it ?

6 Many people heard him speak.

7 Can you explain it to me ?

8 I am going for a walk (in the street).

9 That (length) is a street.

10 Walk, or go by road, (on foot).

' Kom is sometimes Kom². Some people use another word but this one will do for both sounds.

Yeung. A large number of words have a changed sound, which often resembles the second high tone or inflection (see yan₁ in lesson 2 No. 7 etc.)

The Fourth Exercise—(Conversation.)

1 Why do you not go ?
Tim² kaai² nei₂ m₁ hui³ ni¹ ?
點 解 你 唔 去 呢

2 I do not know the way.
Ngoh₂ m₁ shik⁴ lo₃.
我 唔 識 路

3 Do you know how to go to that street ?
Nei₂ shik⁴ hui³ koh² t'iu² kaai¹ m₁ ni¹ ?
你 識 去 个 條 街 唔 呢

4 You explain to me how to go
Nei₂ kaai² ngoh₂ t'eng¹ tim² *yeung₃ hui³
你 解 我 聽 點 樣 去

5 This is the way to that street.
Koh² t'iu₁ kaai¹ hai₃ kom² *yeung₃ hui³.
个 條 街 係 咁 樣 去

6 Yes, I know.
Kom² *yeung₃ ngoh₂ chi¹.
咁 樣 我 知

7 So you know the way, is that so ?
Kom² nei₂ shik⁴ lo₃, hai₃ m₁ hai₃ ni¹ ?
咁 你 識 路, 係 唔 係 呢

8 Yes, I know now that you have told me.
Hai₃, nei₂ kong² ngoh₂ chi¹, ngoh₂ shik⁴ lo₃.
係, 你 講 我 知, 我 識 路

9 What am I to go to that street for ?
Hui³ koh² t'iu₁ kaai¹ tso₃ mat⁴ ye₂ ni¹ ?
去 个 條 街 做 乜 野 呢

10 You are to go to buy many things.
Hui³ koh² t'iu₁ kaai¹ maai₂ ho² toh¹ ye₂.
去 个 條 街 買 好 多 野

THE FIFTH LESSON

第 五 課—Tai₃ ng₂ foh⁵

1	邊	Pin¹—*Which, who, what, side.*		**6**	茶	Ch'a₁—*Tea.*
2	處	Shue³ (ch'ue⁵)—*Place.*		**7**	菜	Ts'oi³—*Vegetable, food.*
3	食	Shik₄—*Eat, food.*		**8**	飲	Yam²—*Drink.*
4	飯	Faan₃—*Rice, food, meal.*		**9**	完	Uen₁—*Finished, (past tense).*
5	未	Mei₁—*Yet, not yet.*		**10**	肉	Yuk₄—*Flesh, meat.*

1 佢見邊个人呢. K'ui₂ kin' pin¹ koh' yan₁ ni¹ ?

2 嚟呢處. Lai₁ m¹ shue³.

3 我要食的野. Ngoh₂ iu⁵ shik₄ ti¹ ye₂.

4 係食飯唔係. Hai₃ shik₄ faan₃ m₁ hai₃.

5 你食飯未. Nei₂ shik₄ faan₃ mei₃ ?

6 有啲茶係好. Yau₂ ti¹ ch'a₁ hai₃ ho².

7 去邊處買菜呢. Hui⁵ pin¹ shue⁵ maai₂ ts'oi³ ni¹?

8 我食飯, 唔飲茶. Ngoh₂ shik₄ faan₃, m₁ yam² ch'a₁.

9 佢食完飯未. Kui₂ shik₄ uen₁ faan₃ mei₃ ?

10 食肉好唔好呢. Shik₄ yuk₄ ho² m₁ ho² ni¹ ?

1 What man did he see ?

2 Come here.

3 I want to eat something (food).

4 Is it rice you are eating.

5 Have you had (rice) your meal yet ?

6 Some tea is good.

7 Where do you go to buy vegetables.

8 I will eat rice and not drink tea.

9 Has he finished his meal yet?

10 Is it good to eat meat ?

The Fifth Exercise --(Conversation.)

1 Do you know where he has gone ?

Nei₂ chi¹ k'ui₂ hui³ pin¹ shue³ m₁ chi¹ ni¹ ?

你 知 佢 去 邊 處 唔 知 呢 ?

2 How do I know where he has gone ?

Ngoh₂ tim² chi¹ k'ui₂ hui³ pin¹ shue³ ni¹ ?

我 點 知 佢 去 邊 處 呢．

3 I saw him go to that street to buy things.

Ngoh₂ kin' k'ui₂ hui³ koh² t'iu₂ kaai¹ maai₂ ye₂.

我 見 佢 去 个 條 街 買 野

4 What did he go to buy ?

Hui' maai₂ mat⁴ ye₂

去 買 乜 野

5 He is buying vegetables and meat, a little of each.

Maai₂ ti¹ ts'oi³, maai₂ ti¹ yuk₄, yat⁴ yeung₃ maai₂ ti¹.

買 啲 菜, 買 啲 肉, 一 樣 買 啲

6 Is there nothing much to be bought in that street ?

Koh² t'iu₂ kaai¹ hai₃ m₁ hai₃ mo₂ mat⁴ ye₂ maai₂ ni¹ ?

个 條 街 係 唔 係 冇 乜 野 買 呢

7 No, there are many things to be bought in that street.

M₁ hai₂, koh² t'iu₂ kaai¹ maai₂ tak⁴ ho² toh¹ ye₂

唔 係, 个 條 街 買 得 好 多 野

8 What will you do after your meal ?

Nei₂ shik₄ uen₁ faan₃ tso₃ mat⁴ ye₂ ?

你 食 完 飯 做 乜 野

9 After I have finished my meal (rice) I will go to see two men

Ngoh₂ shik₄ uen₁ faan₃ iu³ hui³ kin¹ leung₂ koh² yan₁.

我 食 完 飯 要 去 見 兩 个 人

10 Do not go to see them till they have had their meal (rice).

K'ui₂ mei₃ shik₄ uen₁ faan₃, nei₂ m₁ ho⁴ hui³ kin' k'ui₂.

佢 未 食 完 飯, 你 唔 好 去 見 佢

THE SIXTH LESSON

第 六 課—Tai₃ luk₄ foh³

1	喺	Hai²—*To be in, or at, a place.*	6	同	T'ung₁—*With, and, same*
2	時	Shi₁—*Time, an hour*	7	鐵	T'it₀—*Iron.*
3	工	Kung¹—*Work.*	8	就	Tsau₃—*Then, soon, thus*
4	打	Ta²—*Beat, do.*	9	鐘	Chung¹—*Clock, time*
5	錢	*Ts'in₁—*Money, cash*	10	想	Seung²—*Desire, wish.*

1 佢喺邊處. K'ui₂ hai¹ pin¹ shue³ ?

    1 Where is he ?

2 我時時食菜. Ngoh₂ shi₁ shi₁ shik₄ ts'oi³.

    2 I always eat vegetables.

3 你做乜野工. Nei₂ tso₃ mat⁴ ye₂ kung¹ ?

    3 What work do you do ?

4 我做打銀. Ngoh₂ tso₃ ta² *ngan₁.

    4 I am a silver smith.

5 幾多个銀錢. Kei² toh¹ koh³ ngan₁ *ts'in₁.

    5 How many dollars ?

6 邊个同佢去. Pin¹ koh³ t'ung₁ k'ui₂ hui⁵ ?

    6 Who went with him?

7 呢條鐵唔係幾好. Ni¹ t'iu₁ t'it₀ m₁ hai₃ kei² ho².

    7 This piece of iron is not very good.

8 我就同佢去. Ngoh₂ tsau₃ t'ung₁ k'ui₂ hui⁵.

    8 I will go with him (soon).

9 你幾時去買鐘呢. Nei₂ kei² shi₁ hui³ maai₂ chung¹ ni² ?

    9 When are you going to buy a clock ?

10 佢想唔嚟. Kui₂ seung² m₁ lai₁.

    10 He does not want to come.

The Sixth Exercise—(Conversstion.)

1 Where do you werk ?

Nei₂ hai² pin¹ shue³ tso⸱ kung¹ ni¹ ?

你 喺 邊 處 做 工 呢.

2 I work there.

Ngoh, hai' koh² shue⁷ tso₃ kung¹.

我 喺 個 處 做 工

3 Do you always work there ?

Nei₂ shi₁ shi₁ hai² koh² shue⁹ tso⸱ hai⸱ m₁ hai₃ ?

你 時 時 喺 個 處 做 係 唔 係

4 Sometimes (yes) I work there, and sometimes (no) not.

Yau₂ shi₁ hai⸱, vau₂ shi₁ m₁ hai⸱.

有 時 係, 有 時 唔 係.

5 Can you go with me to buy a clock ?

T'ung₁ ngoh₂ hui⸀ maai₂ yat⁴ koh³ chung¹ tak⁴ m₁ tak⁴ ni¹.

同 我 去 買 一 個 鈍 得 唔 得 呢

6 Where are you going to buy it ?

Hui⸀ pin¹ shue³ maai₂ ni¹ ?

去 邊 處 買 呢.

7 There are some in that street.

Koh² t'iu₁ kaai¹ yau₂ (lok₀).

個 條 街 有 (咯)

8 When will you come to go with me ?

Nei₂ kei² *shi₁ lai₁ t'ung₁ ngoh₂ hui⸀ ni¹ ?

你 幾 時 嚟 同 我 去 呢.

9 I will come presently (soon).

Ngoh₂ tsau₃ lai₁.　我 就 嚟

10 What price do you want to pay ?

Maai₁ kei² toh¹ *ngan₁ yat⁴ koh³ ni¹ ?

買 幾 多 銀 一 *個 呢

11 Six dollars would be good.

Luk₄ koh³ ngan₁ *ts'in₁ tsau₃ ho².

六 個 銀 錢 就 好.

12 You cannot buy a good one for as little as six dollars.

Luk₄ koh³ ngan₁ *ts'in₁ kom³ shiu², m₁ maai₂ tak⁴ ho² ye₂.

六 個 銀 錢 咁 少, 唔 買 得 好 野

個 is the same as 个

THE SEVENTH LESSON

第 七 課—Tai, ts'at⁴ foh°

1　間　Kaan¹—*A classifier for house, a house.*
　　　Kaan`—*To partition.*

2　屋　Uk⁴—*A house, building.*

3　用　Yung,—*To use, useful, use.*

4　叫　Kiu`—*To call, to tell.*

5　嘅　Ke³—*Sign of possessive, a terminating particle.*

6　日　Yat,—*Sun, day.*

7　月　Uet,—*Moon, month.*

8　今　Kam¹—*Now, to-day.*

9　昨　Tsok,—*(With day), yesterday, last.*

10　番(返)　Faan¹ (faan²) — *Return, come back*

1　呢間係乜野. Ni¹ kaan¹ hai, mat⁴ ye,?

1　What is this (house) kaan ?

2　个間係屋.　Koh² kaan¹ hai, uk⁴.

2　That is a house.

3　你用乜野食飯. Nei, yung, mat⁴ ye, shik, faan,?

3　What do you use to eat rice with?

4　叫佢嚟. Kiu` k'ui, lai,.

4　Tell him to come.

5　啲錢係乜野做嘅.　Ti¹ *ts'in, hai, mat⁴ ye, tso, ke° ?

5　What are the coins made of ?

6　日日要做好多工.　Yat, yat, iu`tso, ho² toh¹ kung¹.

6　I have a lot of work to do every day.

7　呢个係幾月呢, Ni¹ koh° hai, kei² uet, ni¹ ?

7　What month is this ?

8　我想今日去佢處. Ngoh, seung' kam¹ yat, hui³ k'ui, shue³.

8　I want to go to his place today.

9　昨日冇人嚟. Tsok, yat, mo, yan, lai,.

9　No one came yesterday.

10　你幾時番嚟? Nei, kei² *shi, faan¹ lai,.

10　When will you come back.

The Seventh Exercise—(Conversation.)

1 Whose houses are these ?
Ni¹ kei² kaan¹ uk⁴ hai, pin¹ koh³ ke³ ?
呢 幾 間 屋 係 邊 个 嘅 ?

2 These houses are mine.
Ni¹ kei² kaan¹ hai, ngoh, ke³.
呢 幾 間 係 我 嘅.

3 When did you buy them ?
Nei, kei⁴ *shi₁ maai₁ ke⁵ ni¹ ?
你 幾 時 買 嘅 呢.

4 I bought them several months ago.
Ngoh, maai₁ yau₂ kei² koh° uet₄ (lok₀).
我 買 有 幾 个 月 (咯).

5 You did not ask me to buy for you.
Nei, m₁ kiu³ ngoh₂ t'ung₁ nei₂ maai₂.
你 唔 叫 我 同 你 買.

6 Yesterday, I was told that you buy houses.
Tsok₄ yat₄ yau₂ yan₁ wa₃ ngoh₂ chi¹ nei₂ maai₂ uk⁴.
昨 日 有 人 話 我 知, 你 買 屋.

7 Did you not know I buy them ?
Nei₂ m, chi¹ ngoh₂ maai₂ (*me¹!) ?
你 唔 知 我 買 (咩!)

8 How could I know ?
Ngoh, tim² chi¹ ni¹ ?
我 點 知 呢 ?

9 I have not seen you for many months.
Ngoh, ho² toh¹ koh³ uet₄ m₁ kin³ nei₂.
我 好 多 个 月 唔 見 你.

10 I was away elsewhere, and came back to day.
Ngoh₂ hui³ tai, i, shue³, kam¹ yat₄ faan¹ lai,.
我 去 第 二 處, 今 日 番 嚟.

Me¹ at the end of a sentence is an interrogative sound.

THE EIGHTH LESSON

第 八 課—Tai₃ paat₀ foh³

1	話	Wa,—*Speak, say, tell.*	6	使	Shai²—*To use, need.*
2	大	Taai—*Large, great.*	7	至	Chi³—*To, to come to.*
3	細	Sai'—*Small.*	8	陣	Chan—*A classifier, a short time.*
4	賣	Maai₃—*Sell.*	9	前	Ts'in₁—*In front, formerly.*
5	都	To¹—*Also.*	10	後	Hau₃—*Behind, after*

1 有人話要去買野. Yau₂ yan₁ wa₃ iu² hui¹ maai₂ ye₂.

2 佢去大街買野. K'ui₂ hui¹ taai₃ kaai¹ maai₂ ye₂.

3 佢買啲好細嘅野. K'ui₂ maai₂ ti¹ ho² sai³ ke³ ye₂.

4 佢想賣一間屋. K'ui₂ seung² maai₃ yat⁴ kaan¹ uk⁴.

5 佢賣做得,買都做得. K'ui₂ maai₃ tso₃ tak⁴, maai, to¹ tso₃ tak⁴.

6 佢時時使好多銀. K'ui₂ shi₁ shi₁ shai² ho² toh¹ *ngan₁.

7 佢話要有錢至得. K'ui₂ wa₃ iu³ yau₂ *ts'in₁ chi³ tak⁴.

8 佢一陣就去飲茶. K'ui₂ yat⁴ chan₀ tsau₃ hui³ yam² ch'a₁.

9 我前日去聽人講野. Ngoh₂ ts'in₁ yat₄ hui³ t'eng¹ yan₁ kong² ye₂.

10 後來我同个人行街. Hau₃ loi₁ ngoh₂ t'ung₃ koh³ yan₁ haang₁ kaai¹.

1 A man says he must go to buy things.

2 He went to the big street to buy things.

3 He bought some very little things.

4 He wants to sell a house.

5 He can sell, and can also buy.

6 He always uses a great deal of money'

7 He said he must have money.

8 He will go soon (in a moment) to drink tea.

9 Two days ago, I went to hear a man talking.

10 Afterwards I went with the man for a walk in the street.

The Eighth Exercise—(Conversation.)

1 Did you say some people tell lies ?

Nei₂ wa₁ yau₂ yan₁ kong² taai₃ wa₃, hai₃ m₁ hai ?

你 話 有 人 講 大 話, 係 唔 係 ?

2 Yes, I said some people tell lies.

Hai₃, ngoh₂ wa₃ yau₂ yan₁ kong² taai₃ wa₃.

係, 我 話 有 人 講 大 話.

3 Have you heard people tell lies ?

Nei₂ yau₂ t'eng¹ yan₁ kong² taai₃ wa₃ mo₂ ni¹ ?

你 有 聽 人 講 大 話 冇 呢.

4 Yes, I have heard people tell lies.

Yau₂, ngoh₂ yau₂ t'eng¹ yan₁ kong² taai₃ wa₃.

有, 我 有 聽 人 講 大 話.

5 When did you hear him speak (lies).

Nei₂ kei² *shi₁ t'eng¹ k'ui₂ kong².

你 幾 時 聽 佢 講

6 I hear people talk (lies) every day.

Ngoh₁ yat₄ yat₄ to¹ t'eng¹ yan₁ kong².

我 日 日 都 聽 人 講.

7 Are there so many people who tell lies ?

Yau₂ kom³ toh¹ yan₁ kong² taai₃ wa₃, hai₃ m₁ hai₃ ni¹ ?

有 咁 多 人 講 大 話, 係 唔 係 呢.

8 Yes, everyone tells lies, in a moment one may do it.

Hai₃, yan₁ yan₁ yau₂ kong², yat⁴ chan₃ tsau₃ kong²

係, 人 人 有 講, 一 陣 就 講.

9 The day before yesterday I heard some one say so.

Ts'in₁ yat₄ ngoh₂ to¹ t'eng¹ yan₁ kom² kong².

前 日 我 都 聽 人 咁 講.

10 Everyone knows that.

Koh² ti¹ yan₁ yan₁ to¹ chi¹.

个 啲 人 人 都 知.

香港‧澳門雙城成長經典

THE NINTH LESSON

第 九 課—Tai₃ kau² foh³

1	俾	Pei'—*Give, allow.*	6	出	Ch'ut⁴—*Out, go out.*
2	水	Shui²—*Water.*	7	入	Yap₄—*Enter, in.*
3	火	Foh²—*Fire.*	8	半	Poon³—*Half.*
4	耐	Noi,—*Long time, patience.*	9	年	Nin₁—*Year.*
5	柴	Ch'aai,—*Wood, firewood.*	10	等	Tang²—*Wait, a class or type.*

1 俾啲茶我飲. Pei² ti¹ ch'a₁ ngoh, yam².

2 飲水好唔好呢. Yam² shui² ho² m, ho¹ ni¹ ?

3 飲水係好,飲火水唔好. Yam² shui² hai₃ ho², yam² foh² shui² m, ho².

4 我聽人講好耐. Ngoh₂ t'eng¹ van, kong² ho² noi₃.

5 多人用火柴. Toh¹ yan, yung₃ foh² ch'aai,.

6 有人出街行冇呢. Yau₂ yan, ch'ut⁴ kaai¹ haang, mo₂ ni¹ ?

7 有, 好多人出出入入. Yau₂, ho² toh¹ yan, ch'ut⁴ ch'ut⁴ yap₄ yap₄.

8 有人打半日工. Yau₂ yan, ta² poon³ vat₄ kung¹.

9 我做工幾年咁耐. Ngoh₂ tso₃ kung¹ kei² nin, kom³ noi₃.

10 我等上工一年咁耐. Ngoh, tang² sheung₂ kung¹ yat⁴ nin, kom³ noi₃.

1 Give me some tea to drink.

2 Is it good to drink water?

3 Water is good to drink, kerosene is not.

4 I heard people say it long ago.

5 Many people use matches.

6 Have any people gone for a walk (in the street)?

7 Yes, many people are going in and out.

8 Some people work for half the day.

9 I have worked for some years.

10 I have waited for work for a year.

The Ninth Exercise—(Conversation.)

1   Where have you been so long ;
     Nei$_2$ hui^3 pin^1 shue^3 kom^3 noi$_3$?
        你 去 邊 處 咁 耐

2   I went away to work for a long time.
     Ngoh$_2$ ch'ut^4 hui^3 ta^2 kung^1 ho^2 noi$_3$.
        我 出 去 打 工 好 耐.

3   How long have you been away ?
     Nei$_2$ hui^3 yau$_2$ kei^2 *noi$_3$
        你 去 有 幾 耐.

4   I went away for several years.
     Ngoh$_2$ hui^3 kei^2 nin$_1$ kom^3 noi$_3$.
        我 去 幾 年 咁 耐.

5   What work did you go to do ?
     Nei$_2$ hui^3 tso$_3$ mat^4 ye$_2$ kung^1 ni^1 ?
        你 去 做 乜 野 工 呢.

6   I went away as a silversmith.
     Ngoh$_2$ hui ta^2 *ngan$_1$.
        我 去 打 銀.

7   Have you been a blacksmith ?
     Yau$_2$ mo$_2$ ta^2 t'it$_8$?
        有 冇 打 鐵

8   No, I cannot do blacksmith's work.
     Mo$_2$, ngoh$_2$ m$_1$ shik^4 ta^2 t'it$_8$.
        冇, 我 唔 識 打 鐵

9   Now you are back, need you go again ?
     Ni^1 chan$_3$ faan^1 lai$_1$ m$_1$ shai^2 hui^3 hai$_8$ m$_1$ hai$_8$?
        呢 陣 番 嚟 唔 使 去 係 唔 係.

10   I want to go about (in and out), and wait till next year to go.
     Ngoh$_2$ seung^2 ch'ut^4 ch'ut^4 yap$_4$ yap$_4$, tang^2 ch'ut^4 *nin$_1$ chi^8 hui^3.
        我 想 出 出 入 入, 等 出 年 至 去

THE TENTH LESSON

第 十 課—Tai₅ shap₄ foh³

1	烟	In¹—*Smoke, tobacco*		6	估	Koo²—*Think, guess*	
2	仔	Tsai²—*Boy, small*		7	怕	P'a³—*Fear, think, (afraid)*	
3	理	Lei₂—*Manage, control, principle*		8	明	Ming₁, meng₁—*Clear, bright, understand*	
4	事	Sz₃—*Affairs, business, matters*		9	白	Paak₂—*White, clear*	
5	到	To³—*To come to, arrive*		10	住	Chue₃—*Dwell, live, (present tense, continuous)*	

1 你食烟唔食. Nei₂ shik₄ in¹ m₁ shik₄.

2 烟仔就食. In¹ tsai² tsau₃ shik₄.

3 唔好理咁多野. M₁ ho² lei₂ kom' toh¹ ye₂.

4 日日都有好多事做. Yat₄ yat₄ to¹ yau₂ ho² toh¹ sz₃ tso₃.

5 佢幾時到呢. K'ui₂ kei² *shi₁ to° ni¹ ?

6 我估都係呢幾日就到. Ngoh₂ koo² to¹ hai₁ ni¹ kei² yat₄ tsau₃ to³.

7 使乜怕呢? Shai² mat⁴ p'a³ ni¹ ?

8 明日同你去. Ming₁ yat₄ t'ung₁ nei₂ hui˙.

9 明白唔呢. Ming₁ paak₄ m₁ ni¹ ?

10 你喺邊處住呢. Nei₂ hai² pin¹ shue³ chue₃ ni¹ ?

1 Do you smoke (tobacco) or not ?

2 I smoke (eat) cigarettes.

3 Do not attend to so many things.

4 Every day I have many things to do.

5 When did (or will) he arrive ?

6 I think he will be here during these few days.

7 Why are you afraid ?

8 I will go with you to-morrow.

9 Do you understand ?

10 Where do you live ?

The Tenth Exercise—(Conversation.)

1 When you were young did you smoke cigarettes ?

Nei₂ sai⁴ koh³ koh² shi₁ yau₂ shik₄ in¹ tsai² mo₂ ni¹ ?

你 細 個 個 時 有 食 烟 仔 冇 呢

2 No, when one is young, one cannot smoke.

Mo₂, sai⁵ koh³ koh² shi₁ m₁ shik₄ tak⁴ in¹.

冇, 細 個 個 時 唔 食 得 烟

3 Why can he not smoke ?

Tim² kaai² m₁ shik₄ tak⁴ ni¹ ?

點 解 唔 食 得 呢

4 At that time, one is afraid of many things.

Koh² chan₄ shi₁ p'a³ ho² toh¹ yeung₃ ye₂ ke³.

個 陣 時 怕 好 多 樣 野 嘅

5 What good is smoking ?

Shik₄ in¹ yau₂ mat⁴ ho² ch'ue³ ni¹ ?

食 烟 有 乜 好 處 呢

6 I do not smoke and cannot tell the good of it ?

Ngoh, mo, shik₄ in¹, wa₄ m₁ ch'ut⁴ yau₂ mat⁴ ho² shue³.

我 冇 食 烟, 話 唔 出 有 乜 好 處

7 Some people smoke when very small (young).

Yau₂ ti¹ yan₁ ho² sai¹ koh³ tsau₃ shik₄ in¹.

有 啲 人 好 細 個 就 食 烟

8 I do not understand why they are allowed to.

Ngoh₂ to¹ m₁ ming₁ paak₄ tim² kaai² pei² k'ui₂ shik₄ ni¹.

我 都 唔 明 白 點 解 俾 佢 食 呢.

9 I (also) cannot attend to so many things.

Ngoh₂ to¹ m₁ lei₂ tak⁴ kom⁵ toh¹ sz₃.

我 都 唔 理 得 咁 多 事.

10 If you want to, you cannot control them.

Seung² lei₂ to¹ lei₂ m₁ to³ ke³.

想 理 都 理 唔 到 嘅

11 I do not like listening to so many things.

Ngoh₂ ho² p'a³ t'eng¹ kom² toh¹ ye₂.

我 好 怕 聽 咁 多 野

12 You need not listen unless you like.

Nei₂ m₁ t'eng¹ to¹ tak⁴ ke³.   你 唔 聽 都 得 嘅

ᵇ Shue³ is sometimes spoken as ch'ue⁵.

THE ELEVENTH LESSON

第十一課—Tai₃ shap₄ yat⁴ foh³

1	黃	Wong₁—*Yellow, a surname, Mr. Wong.*
2	色	Shik⁴—*Colour.*
3	黑	Hak⁴—*Black.*
4	擰	Ning¹—*Bring, fetch.*
5	攞	Loh²—*Get, bring here.*
6	企	K'ei₂—*To stand, used for residence, home.*
7	門	Moon₁—*Door.*
8	開	Hoi¹—*Open.*
9	閂	Shaan¹—*Shut, and fasten.*
10	定	Teng₃—*Arrange, determine, fix, or.*

1 呢間係黃屋. Ni¹ kaan¹ hai₃ wong₁ uk⁴.

2 要乜野色呢 Iu³ mat⁴ ye₂ shik⁴ ni¹?

3 黑色都好. Hak⁴ shik⁴ to¹ ho².

4 擰去我嘅屋. Ning¹ hui³ ngoh₂ ke³ uk⁴.

5 攞多少銀嚟. Loh² toh¹ shiu² *ngan₁ lai₁.

6 做乜你企呢. Tso₃ mat⁴ nei₂ k'ei₂ ni¹?

7 有人打門. Yau₂ yan₁ ta² moon₁

8 等我去開. Tang² ngoh₂ hui³ hoi¹.

9 閂好門未. Shaan¹ ho² moon₁ mei₃?

10 開定唔開. Hoi¹ teng₃ m₁ hoi¹?

1 This house is a yellow (coloured) house.

2 What colour do you want?

3 A dark (colour) will do (be good).

4 Take it to my house.

5 Bring some money (a little), (more or less).

6 Why are you standing?

7 Some one is knocking at the door.

8 I will go and open it, (let me, or wait till I open it)

9 Have you fastened the door yet?

10 Shall I open it or not?

The Eleventh Exercise—(Conversation.)

1 Who is knocking (at the door) ?
Pin^1 koh^3 ta^2 moon$_1$? 邊 个 打 門

2 I knocked.
Ngoh$_2$ ta^2 moon$_1$ 我 打 門

3 Who are you ?
Nei$_2$ hai$_3$ mat^4 *yan$_1$? 你 係 乜 人

4 I am Wong$_1$ Hoi^1 (Hoi^1 is the name, Wong the surname).
Ngoh$_2$ hai$_3$ Wong$_1$ Hoi^1. 我 係 黃 開

5 Why have you come ?
Nei$_2$ lai$_1$ tso$_5$ mat^4 ye$_2$ ni^1 ? 你 嚟 做 乜 野 呢

6 I came to take some things away (back).
Ngoh$_2$ lai$_1$ ning^1 ti^1 ye$_2$ faan^1 hui^5.
我 嚟 擰 啲 野 返 去.

7 Go in and take them (can).
Yap$_4$ hui^5 loh^2 tsau$_3$ tak^4. 入 去 攞 就 得

8 After taking them, we must fasten the door again.
Loh^2 uen$_1$ ngoh$_2$ tei$_3$ iu^3 shaan^1 faan^1 moon$_1$ chi^5 ho^2.
攞 完 我 哋 要 閂 番 門 至 好

9 It is so dark, I do not know how to fasten it
Kom^3 hak^4 m$_1$ shik^4 shaan^1.
咁 黑 唔 識 閂

10 Tell Ts'in Yung to do it for you (Yung name, Ts'in
Kiu^5 Ts'in$_1$ Yung. t'ung$_1$ nei$_2$ shaan^1.   [surname.)
叫 錢 用 同 你 閂

11 Why is he away so long ? (not come back).
Kom^3 noi$_3$ k'ui$_2$ to^1 m$_1$ faan^1 lai$_1$
咁 耐 佢 都 唔 番 嚟

12 He has not fixed any time to be back.
K'ui$_2$ m$_1$ teng$_3$ kei^2 shi$_1$ faan^1 lai$_1$
佢 唔 定 幾 時 番 嚟

香港・澳門雙城成長經典

第 十 二 課—Tai₃ Shap₄ i foh³

1	成	Shing₁—*Complete.*		
2	百	Paak₀—*One hundred, all.*		
3	千	Ts'in¹—*One thousand.*		
4	落	Lok₄—*Down, to go down*		
5	雨	Ue₂—*Rain.*		
6	頭	T'au₁—*Head, top.*		
7	隻	Cheko — *Classifier for animals, etc.*		
8	手	Shau⁰—*Hand.*		
9	脚	Keuk₀—*Foot.*		
10	天	T'in¹—*Heaven, sky.*		

1 你成日去邊處呢. Nei₂ shing₁ yat₄ hui³ pin¹ shue³ ni¹?

1 Where do you go all day?

2 個處有百幾人. Koh² shue³ yau₂ paak₀ kei² yan₁.

2 There are more than 100 people there.

3 十個百係一千. Shap₄ koh³ paak₀ hai₃ yat⁴ t'sin¹.

3 Ten hundreds make one thousand.

4 我要落去. Ngoh₂ iu³ lok₄ hui³.

4 I must go down.

5 昨日成日落雨. Tsok₄ yat₄ shing₁ yat₄ lok₄ ue₂.

5 Yesterday, it rained all day.

6 有日頭冇. Yau₂ yat₄ *t'au₁ mo₂?

6 Is there any sun (shining).

7 呢隻係乜野呢. Ni¹ chek₀ hai₃ mat⁴ ye₂ ni¹?

7 What is this (chek₀) thing.

8 個隻係手. Koh² chek₀ hai₃ shau².

8 That (chek₀) is a hand.

9 人人有手有脚. Yan₁ yan₁ yau₂ shau² yau₂ keuk₀.

9 Everyone has hands and feet.

10 今日天時幾好 Kam¹ yat₄ t'in¹ shi₁ kei² ho².

10 To-day the weather is (fairly) quite good.

英粵通語 Cantonese for everyone ——香港大學粵語教材（一九三一）

The Twelfth Exercise—(Conversation.)

1 When do you think it will rain ?

Nei₂ koo² kei² *shi₁ yau₂ ue₂ lok₄ ni¹ ?

你 估 幾 時 有 雨 落 呢

2 The weather is so good to day, how can one know when rain will come.

Kam¹ yat₄ t'in¹ shi₁ kom¹ ho², tim² chi¹ kei² shi₁ yau₂ ue₂ lok₄.

今 日 天 時 咁 好, 點 知 幾 時 有 雨 落

3 Is rain good or not ?

Lok₄ ue₂ ho² m₁ ho² ni¹? 落 雨 好 唔 好 呢

4 Sometimes it is good, sometimes it is bad.

Yau₂ shi₁ ho², yau₂ shi₁ m₁ ho².

有 時 好, 有 時 唔 好

5 Well, when is it good ?

Kom² *yeung₃ kei² shi₁ chi⁴ ho² ni¹ ?

咁 樣, 幾 時 至 好 呢

6 When it is needed it is good, when not needed it is bad.

Iu³ yung₃ koh² shi₁ tsau₃ ho², m₁ iu³ yung₂ tsau₂ m₁ ho².

要 用 個 時 就 好, 唔 要 用 就 唔 好

7 Can he walk (or not) when it is raining ?

Lok₁ ue₂ koh² shi₁ k'ui₂ haang₁ tak⁴ m₁ haang₁ tak⁴ ni¹ ?

落 雨 個 時 佢 行 得 唔 行 得 呢

8 He can't. He cannot walk when it is raining.

M₁ tak⁴, lok₄ ue₂ koh² shi₁ k'ui₂ m₁ haang₁ tak⁴.

唔 得, 落 雨 個 時 佢 唔 行 得

9 Why cannot he walk ?

Tim² kaai² m₁ haang₁ tak⁴ ni¹ ?

點 解 唔 行 得 呢

10 There is something (wrong) with his foot.

K'ui₂ chek₀ keuk₀ yau₂ sz₃, 佢 隻 脚 有 事

11 Has he asked some one to attend to it ?

Yau₂ kiu³ yan₁ ta² lei₂ mo₂ ? 有 叫 人 打 理 冇

12 Yes, every day he gets a person to attend to it.

Yau₂, yat₄ yat₄ to¹ yau₂ kiu³ yan₁ ta² lei₂.

有, 日 日 都 有 叫 人 打 理

THE THIRTEENTH LESSON

第 十 三 課—Tai₅ shap₄ saam¹ foh³

1	面	Min₃ — *Face, surface, the top.*	6	中	Chung¹—*Middle, centre.*
2	海	Hoi²—*Sea, Ocean.*	7	外	Ngoi₃—*Outside.*
3	青	Ts'ing¹—*Green, blue, clear.*	8	過	Kwoh⁵—*Pass, over, past, finished.*
4	西	Sai¹—*West.*	9	山	Shaan¹—*Mountain, hills*
5	國	Kwok₀—*Country, nation.*	10	睇	T'ai²—*See, observe, look.*

1 你个面有點黑野. Nei₂ koh' min₃ yau₂ tim² hak⁴ ye₂.

   1 Your face has a spot of black on it.

2 有人落海. Yau₂ yan₁ lok₄ hoi².

   2 Some people went (down) into the sea.

3 海水係青色. Hoi² shui² hai₃ ts'ing¹ shik⁴.

   3 Seawater is a bluish colour.

4 佢係西人. K'ui₂ hai₃ sai¹ yan₁.

   4 He is a Westerner, (foreigner).

5 有啲國大, 有啲國細. Yau₂ ti¹ kwok₀ taai₃, yau₂ ti¹ kwok₀ sai³.

   5 Some countries are large, and some small.

6 中國有好多人. Chung¹ kwok₀ yau₂ ho² toh¹ yan₁.

   6 China has many people.

7 呢啲係外國野. Ni¹ ti¹ hai₃ ngoi₃ kwok₀ ye₂.

   7 These are foreign things.

8 今日我要過海. Kam¹ yat₄ ngoh, iu⁵ kwoh⁰ hoi².

   8 To-day I must cross the sea (harbour).

9 山邊冇乜人行. Shaan¹ pin¹ mo₂ mat⁴ yan₁ haang₁.

   9 Not many people walk on the hill side.

10 你睇乜野呢. Nei₂ t'ai² mat⁴ ye₂ ni¹ ?

   10 What are you looking at ?

The Thirteenth Exercise—(Conversation.)

1 Have you been to foreign countries yet ?

Nei₂ yau₂ hui³ kwoh³ ngoi₃ kwok₀ mei₃ ni¹ ?

你 有 去 過 外 國 未 呢

2 I have been to many countries.

Ngoh₂ hui¹ kwoh³ ho² tch¹ kwok₀.

我 去 過 好 多 國

3 Do you know foreign languages or not ?

Nei₂ shik⁴ kong² ngoi₃ kwok₀ *wa₃ m₂ shik⁴ ?

你 識 講 外 國 話 唔 識

4 I can talk a little.

Ngoh₂ shik⁴ kong² toh¹ shiu². 我 識 講 多 少

5 What is there to see in foreign countries ?

Hai² ngoi₃ kwok₀ yau₂ mat⁴ ye₂ t'ai² ni¹ ?

喺 外 國 有 乜 野 睇 呢

6 There are many things to see in foreign countries.

Hai² ngoi₃ kwok₀ yau₂ ho² toh¹ ye₂ t'ai².

喺 外 國 有 好 多 野 睇

7 Are the things there, the same as those here ?

Koh² shue³ ti¹ ye₂ t'ung₁ ni¹ shue³ ti¹ ye₂ t'ung₁ m₂ t'ung₁ ni¹ ?

个 處 啲 野 同 呢 處 啲 野 同 唔 同 呢

8 Some are like, some are different.

Yau₂ ti¹ t'ung₁, yau₂ ti¹ m₂ t'ung₁.

有 啲 同 有 啲 唔 同

9 How long were you in foreign lands ?

Nei₂ hai² ngoi₃ kwok₀ kei² noi₃ ni¹ ?

你 喺 外 國 幾 耐 呢

10 I was abroad for several years.

Ngoh₂ hai² ngoi₃ kwok₀ kei² nin₁ kom³ noi₃.

我 喺 外 國 幾 年 咁 耐

11 What do the people there do mostly ?

Koh² shue³ ti¹ yan₁ tso₂ mat⁴ ye₂ toh¹ ni¹ ?

个 處 啲 人 做 乜 野 多 呢?

12 There are all kinds, exactly like this place.

Yeung₃ *yeung₃ to¹ yau₂ to¹ hai₃ ni¹ shue³ yat⁴ yeung₃.

樣 樣 都 有, 都 係 呢 處 一 樣

香港・澳門雙城成長經典

THE FOURTEENTH LESSON

第 十 四 課—Tai₃ shap₄ sz³ foh³

1	先	Sin¹—*Before, formerly.*
2	生	Sha¹ng—*Born, life.*
3	教	Kaau²—*To teach.*
4	讀	Tuk₄—*Read.*
5	書	Shue¹—*Book.*
6	寫	Se²—*Write.*
7	字	Tsz₃ (chi₃)—*Characters, words.*
8	曉	Hiu²—*To understand.*
9	樓	*Lau₁—*A floor, storey.*
10	學	Hok₄—*To learn.*

1 佢頭先嚟. K'ui₂ t'au₁ sin¹ lai₁.

1 He came a short time ago.

2 佢係黃先生. K'ui₂ hai₃ wong₁ sin¹ shang¹.

2 He is Mr. Wong.

3 點解你唔 教佢做工呢. Tim² kaai² nei₂ m₁ kaau³ k'ui₂ tso₃ kung¹ ni¹ ?

3 Why do you not teach him to work ?

4 佢讀乜野呢. K'ui₂ tuk₄ mat⁴ ye₂ ni¹ ?

4 What is he reading ?

5 佢讀書. Kui₂ tuk₄ shue¹.

5 He is reading a book.

6 我呢幾日要寫好多野. Ngoh₂ ni¹ kei² yat₄ iu³ se² ho² toh¹ ye₂.

6 These few days, I have to write (many things) a great deal.

7 邊个教你寫字呢. Pin¹ koh³ kaau³ nei₂ se² tsz₃ ni¹?

7 Who teaches you to write ?

8 你曉唔曉呢. Nei₂ hiu² m₁ hiu² ni¹ ?

8 Do you understand (or not) ?

9 呢間係寫字樓. Ni¹ kaan¹ hai₃ se² tsz₃ *lau₁.

9 This is the Office.

10 佢學寫字. K'ui₂ hok₄ se² tsz₃.

10 He is learning to write (characters).

英粵通語 Cantonese for everyone ——香港大學粵語教材（一九三一）

The Fourteenth Exercise—(Conversation.)

1 Can you teach me to read, Sir ?
Sin¹ shang¹, kaau₃ ngoh₂ tuk₄ shue¹ tak⁴ m₁ tak⁴ ni¹?
先 生, 教 我 讀 書 得 唔 得 呢?

2 Yes, what books do you want to read ?
Tak⁴, nei₂ seung² tuk₄ mat⁴ ye₂ shue¹ ni¹ ?
得, 你 想 讀 乜 野 書 呢?

3 I want to learn books for daily use.
Ngoh₂ seung² hok₄ ti¹ yat₄ yung₃ ke³ shue¹.
我 想 學 啲 日 用 嘅 書

4 Have you such books ?
Nei₂ yau₂ kom² ke³ shue¹ mo₂ ?
你 有 咁 嘅 書 冇

5 No, I have no such books.
Mo₂, ngoh₂ mo₂ kom² ke³ shue¹.
冇, 我 冇 咁 嘅 書

6 You must buy them.
Nei₂ iu⁶ maai₂ chi³ tak⁴. 你 要 買 至 得

7 Where can I go to buy them ?
Hui³ pin¹ shue³ maai₂ ni¹ ? 去 邊 處 買 呢

8 They are for sale in the first shop in that street.
Koh² t'iu₁ kaai¹ tai₂ yat⁴ kaan¹ tsau₃ yau₂ tak⁴ maai₃.
個 條 街 第 一 間 就 有 得 賣

9 Are there any in the book store at the University ?
Taai₃ hok₄ shue¹ lau₁ yau₂ mo₂ ni¹ ?
大 學 書 樓 有 冇 呢?

10 I think certainly there are.
Ngoh₂ koo² yat⁴ teng₃ yau₂. 我 估 一 定 有

11 Is that library for the use of students ?
Koh² kaan¹ shue¹ lau₁ hai₃ pei² hok₄ shang¹ yung₃ m₁ hai₃?
個 間 書 樓 係 俾 學 生 用 唔 係

12 Yes, the library is for the students to use
Hai₃, kaan¹ shue¹ lau₁ hai₃ pei² hok₄ shang¹ yung₃ ke².
係, 間 書 樓 係 俾 學 生 用 嘅

THE FIFTEENTH LESSON

第 十 五 課—Tai₃ shap₁ ng₂ foh³

1	帶	Taai²—*To lead, bring.*	**6**	熱	It₄—*Hot.*
2	問	Man₃—*To ask.*	**7**	冷	Laang₂—*Cold.*
3	洗	Sai²—*To wash.*	**8**	晚	Maan₂—*Evening, night.*
4	房	*Fong₁—*A room.*	**9**	起	Hei²—*To arise, get up, begin.*
5	身	Shan¹—*The body, one's self.*	**10**	濕	Shap⁴—*Wet.*

1 帶佢嚟我處. Taai³ k'ui₂ lai₁ ngoh₂ shue .

1 Bring him to my place.

2 佢問你有乜野. K'ui₂ man₃ nei₂ yau₂ mat⁴ ye₂ ?

2 He asks, what have you?

3 俾啲水我洗手. Pei² ti¹ shui² ngoh₂ sai² shau².

3 Give me some water to wash my hands.

4 呢間房好多人. Ni¹ kaan¹ *fong₁ ho² toh¹ yan₁.

4 This room has many people (in it).

5 个間係洗身房. Koh² kaan¹ hai₁ sai² shan¹ *fong₁.

5 That room is the bathroom.

6 今日係好熱. Kam¹ yat₄ hai₃ ho˙ it₄.

6 To-day is very hot.

7 天冷要熱水洗身. T'in¹ laang₂ iu˙ it₄ shui² sai² shan¹.

7 In cold weather we need hot water to wash our bodies.

8 前晚我冇睇書. Ts'in₁ maan₂ ngoh₂ mo₂ t'ai² shue¹.

8 The night before last I did not read.

9 佢起身未呢. K'ui₂ hei² shan¹ mei₃ ni¹ ?

9 Has he got up yet ?

10 个條街好濕. Koh² t'iu₁ kaai¹ ho² shap⁴.

10 That street is very wet.

The Fifteenth Exercise—(Conversation.)

1 Which was hotter, to-day or yesterday ?

Kam¹ yat₄ it₄ teng₃ tsok₄ yat₄ it₄ ni¹ ?

今 日 熱 定 昨 日 熱 呢

2 Both days were equally hot ?

Leung₂ yat₄ to¹ hai₃ kom³ it₄ ?

兩 日 都 係 咁 熱

3 What time do you get up in hot weather ?

T'in₁ it₄ nei₂ kei² toh¹ tim² chung¹ hei² shan¹ ni¹ ?

天 熱 你 幾 多 點 鐘 起 身 呢

4 I get up at six o'clock in hot weather.

T'in¹ it₄ ngoh₂ luk₄ tim² hei² shan¹.

天 熱 我 六 點 起 身

5 What have you to do when you get up ?

Hei² shan¹ yau₂ mat⁴ ye₂ tso₃ ni¹ ?

起 身 有 乜 野 做 呢

6 I wash and have a bath when I get up.

Hei² shan¹ sai² min₃ sai² shan¹.   起身洗面洗身.

7 What floor is the bathroom on ?

Sai² shan¹ *fong₁ hai² kei² *lau₁.   洗身房喺幾樓.

8 The bathroom is on the (second) floor.

Sai₂ shan¹ *fong₁ hai² saam¹ *lau₁.

洗 身 房 喺 三 樓

9 Do you need hot water for a bath ?

Iu⁵ it₄ shui² sai² shan¹ m₁ iu⁵ ni¹ ?

要 熱 水 洗 身 唔 要 呢.

10 No, I do not want hot water for a bath.

M₁ iu⁵, ngoh₂ m₁ iu³ it₄ shui² sai² shan¹.

唔 要, 我 唔 要 熱 水 洗 身

11 Why is that bathroom so wet ?

Tim² kaai² koh² kaan¹ sai² shan¹ *fong₁ kom⁵ shap⁴ ni¹ ?

點 解 个 間 洗 身 房 咁 濕 呢

12 I do not know why.

Ngoh₂ to¹ m₁ chi¹ tim² kaai².

我 都 唔 知 點 解

THE SIXTEENTH LESSON

第 十 六 課—Tai₃ shap₄ luk₄ foh³

1	早	Tso²—*Early.*		6	燈	Tang¹—*Lamp.*
2	遲	Ch'i₁—*Late.*		7	快	Faai³—*Quick, happy*
3	夜	Ye₃—*Night, late.*		8	慢	Maan₃—*Slow.*
4	船	Shuen₁—*Ship, boat.*		9	朝	Chiu¹—*Morning.*
5	電	Tin₃—*Electricity, electric.*		10	乾	Kon¹—*Dry.*

1　今早我好早起身. Kam¹ tso² ngoh₂ ho² tso² hei² shan¹.

1 This morning I got up very early.

2　點解你咁遲嚟呢. Tim² kaai² nei₂ kom³ ch'i₁ lai₁ ni¹?

2 Why have you come so late?

3　夜晚有工做. Ye₃ maan₂ yau₂ kung¹ tso₃.

3 I have work to do at night.

4　个隻係夜船. Koh² chek₀ hai₃ ye₃ *shuen₁.

4 That is the night boat.

5　電船仔用好多火水. Tin₃ shuen₁ tsai² yung₃ ho² toh¹ foh² shui².

5 Electric launches use a lot of kerosene.

6　呢間屋有電燈. Ni¹ kaan¹ uk⁴ yau₂ tin₃ tang¹.

6 This house has electric lamps.

7　火船快過電船. Foh² shuen₁ faai³ kwoh³ tin₃ shuen₁.

7 Launches are quicker than electric boats.

8　佢寫字寫得好慢. K'ui₂ se² tsz₃ se² tak⁴ ho² maan₃.

8 He writes very slowly.

9　今朝我未食野. Kam¹ chiu¹ ngoh₂ mei₃ shik₄ ye₂.

9 I have not eaten anything this morning yet.

10　我要買啲乾電. Ngoh₂ iu³ maai₂ ti¹ kon¹ tin₃.

10 I must buy some dry electricity.

The Sixteenth Exercise—(Conversation.)

1 Where are you going so early ?

Nei₂ kom² tso² hui³ pin¹ shue³ ni¹ ?

你 咁 早 去 邊 處 呢

2 I am going on board a boat.

Ngoh₂ hui³ lok₄ shuen₁.　我 去 落 船

3 What time does the boat start ?

Chek₀ shuen₁ kei² toh¹ tim² chung¹ hoi¹ shan¹ ni¹ ?

隻 船 幾 多 點 鐘 開 身 呢

4 It starts at 6.30 a.m.

Luk₄ tim² poon² tsau₃ hoi¹ shan¹.

六 點 半 就 開 身

5 You must go quickly.

Iu⁵ haang₁ faai³ ti¹ chi³ tak⁴.

要 行 快 啲 至 得

6 I need not be so quick, going slower will not be too late.

M₁ shai² kom³ faai³, maan₃ ti¹ mei₃ ch'i₁.

唔 使 咁 快 慢 啲 未 遲

7 Is the day boat quicker or the night boat ?

Yat₄ *shuen₁ faai³ teng₃ (pe₅) ye₃ *shuen₁ faai³ ni¹?

日 船 快 定 夜 船 快 呢

8 Both are equally quick.

Leung₂ chek₀ to¹ hai₃ vat⁴ yeung₁ faai⁵.

兩 隻 都 係 一 樣 快

9 Why is it that the nightboat is sometimes so late ?

Tim² kaai² yau₂ shi₁ ye₃ *shuen₁ kom³ ch'i₁ ni¹

點 解 有 時 夜 船 咁 遲 呢

10 If the tide is out it is late.

Shui² kon¹ tsau₃ ch'i₁ ti¹.　水 乾 就 遲 啲

11 Has the steamer electric bells ?

Foh² shuen₁ yau₂ tin₃ chung¹ mo₂.

火 船 有 電 鐘 冇

12 Yes, the steamer has a large electric bell and a small one.

Yau₂ foh² shuen₁ yau₂ taai₃ tin₃ chung¹ yau₂ sai³ tin₃ chung¹.

有, 火 船 有 大 電 鐘, 有 細 電 鐘

英粵通語 Cantonese for everyone —— 香港大學粵語教材（一九三一）

THE SEVENTEENTH LESSON

第 十 七 課—Tai, shap, ts'at⁴ foh³

1 衫 Shaam¹—*Coat, clothes, dress.*
2 褲 Foo³—*Trousers.*
3 長 Ch'eung₁—*Long.*
4 短 Tuen²—*Short.*
5 舊 Kau₃—*Old.*

6 新 San¹—*New.*
7 件 Kin₃—*Classifier for coat, etc.*
8 淨 Tseng₃—*Clean, only.*
9 尺 Ch'ek₀—*Foot (measure).*
10 寸 Ts'uen¹—*Inch.*

1 你啲衫乾未呢. Nei₂ ti¹ shaam¹ kon¹ mei₃ ni¹ ?
— Are your clothes dry yet ?

2 擰條白褲嚟. Ning¹ t'iu₁ paak₄ foo³ lai₁.
— Bring a pair of white trousers.

3 佢嘅衫長 *過頭. K'ui₂ ke³ shaam¹ ch'eung₁ *kwoh³ t'au₁.
— His coat is too long.

4 黃短褲好睇唔好呢. Wong₁ tuen² foo³ ho² t'ai² m₁ ho² ni¹ ?
— Are yellow short trousers nice to look at ?

5 舊就唔好睇. Kau₃ tsau₃ m₁ ho² t'ai².
— When old they do not look nice.

6 呢間係新屋. Ni¹ kaan¹ hai₂ san¹ uk⁴.
— This is a new house.

7 件件衫都係半新舊. Kin₃ kin₃ shaam¹ to¹ hai₃ poon³ san¹ kau₃.
— All the coats are half old (not very new).

8 我件衫洗得好乾淨. Ngoh₂ kin₃ shaam¹ sai² tak⁴ ho² kon¹ tseng₃.
— My coat has been washed very clean.

9 你有尺冇. Nei₂ yau₂ ch'ek₀ mo₂ ?
— Have you a foot measure ?

10 我條褲三尺一寸長. Ngoh₂ t'iu₁ foo³ saam¹ ch'ek₃ yat⁴ ts'ue³n ch'eung₁.
— My trousers are 3 feet and 1 inch long.

The Seventeenth Exercise—(Conversation.)

1 Who washes your clothes for you ?
Pin¹ koh³ t'ung₁ nei₂ sai² shaam¹ ni¹ ?
邊 个 同 你 洗 衫 呢

2 I give them to some one to wash.
Ngoh₂ pei² yan₁ sai² ke³. 我 俾 人 洗 嘅

3 Do they wash them clean ?
Sai² tak⁴ kon¹ tseng₃ m₁ ni¹ ? 洗 得 乾 淨 唔 呢

4 Fairly clean.
Kei² kon¹ tseng₃. 幾 乾 淨

5 Are they (newly bought) new ?
Hai₃ san¹ maai₂ ke³ m₁ hai₃ ?
係 新 買 嘅 唔 係

6 No, I bought them long ago.
M₁ hai₃, kau₃ shi₁ maai₂ ke³.
唔 係, 舊 時 買 嘅

7 Are long coats good ?
Ch'eung₁ shaam¹ ho² m₁ ho² ni¹ ?
長 衫 好 唔 好 呢

8 Long coats are good.
Ch'eung₁ shaam¹ ho². 長 衫 好

9 Why are they made so short ?
Tim² kaai² tso₅ kom⁵ tuen² ni¹ ?
點 解 做 咁 短 呢

10 If they are too long they do not look well.
Ch'eung₁ *kwoh³ t'au₁ m₁ ho² t'ai².
長 過 頭 唔 好 睇

11 Are the trousers too long ?
Foo³ keuk₀ ch'eung₁ m₁ ch'eung₁ ni¹ ?
褲 脚 長 唔 長 呢

12 A little too long.
Ch'eung₁ yat⁴ ti¹. 長 一 啲

THE EIGHTEENTH LESSON

第 十 八 課—Tai₃ shap₄ paat₀ foh⁵

1	但	Taan₅—*But, only, however.*
2	擠	Chai¹—*To place.*
3	筆	Pat⁴—*Pen, pencil.*
4	枝	Chi¹—*Classifier for pens.*
5	口	Hau²—*Mouth, classifier for a port.*
6	方	Fong¹—*Square, exact, then, place, direction.*
7	†地	Tei₃—*Earth, world, land*
8	上	Sheung₃—*Above, sheung to go up, ascend.*
9	*下	Ha₃—*Below.*
10	檯	*T'oi—*A table.*

---

1 樣樣好, 但呢樣唔好. Yeung₃ *yeung₃ ho², taan₃ ni¹ yeung₃ m₁ ho².

1 Everything is good, but this kind is not good.

2 你擠乜野喺呢處. Nei₂ chai¹ mat⁴ ye₂ hai² ni¹ shue⁵ ?

2 What did you put here?

3 我後朝早去買筆. Ngoh₂ hau₃ chiu¹ tso² hui³ maai₂ pat⁴.

3 I am going to buy pens, the day after tomorrow in the morning.

4 買幾多枝筆呢. Maai₂ kei² toh¹ chi¹ pat⁴ ni¹.

4 How many pens will you buy ?

5 門口有个人. Moon₁ hau³ yau₂ koh³ yan₁.

5 There is a man at the door.

6 呢樣鐵係四方唔係. Ni¹ yeung₃ t'it₀ hai₃ sz³ fong¹ m₁ hai₃.

6 Is this kind of iron square ?

7 佢間屋有好多地方. K'ui₂ kaan¹ uk⁴ yau₂ ho² toh¹ tei₃ fong¹.

7 There is a lot of space in his house.

8 去買啲上等火柴. Hui³ maai₂ ti¹ sheung₃ tang² foh² *ch'aai₁.

8 Go and buy some of the best matches.

9 樓下有洗身房. Lau₁ ha₃ yau₂ sai⁴ shan¹ fong₁.

9 There is a bathroom downstairs.

10 檯上有一枝電燈. *T'oi₁ sheung₃ yau₂ yat⁴ chi¹ tin₃ tang¹.

10 There is an electric lamp on the table.

† 地 With 口 at side is used for plural of pronouns and men.
* 下 with 口 attached means once, or a short time.

The Eighteenth Exercise—(Conversation.)

1 What do you use to write with ?
Nei, yung, mat⁴ ye₂ se² tsz, ni¹ ?
你 用 乜 野 寫 字 呢

2 I use a pen to write with.
Ngoh₂ yung, pat⁴ se² tsz,. 我 用 筆 寫 字

3 Where will you write ?
Hai² pin¹ shue³ se² ni¹ ? 喺 邊 處 寫 呢

4 I will write at the desk.
Hai² se² tsz, *t'oi, se². 喺 寫 字 檯 寫

5 Do you know short hand ?
Nei₂ shik⁴ se² faai³ tsz₃ m, shik⁴ ?
你 識 寫 快 字 唔 識

6 I can do type writing, but do not know short hand.
Ngoh₂ shik⁴ ta² tsz,, taan, hai₂ m, shik⁴ se² faai¹ tsz₃.
我 識 打 字, 但 係 唔 識 寫 快 字

7 Who taught you type writing ?
Pin¹ koh³ kaau³ nei₂ ta² tsz₃ ni¹ ?
邊 個 教 你 打 字 呢

8 A westerner taught me type writing.
Yat⁴ koh³ sai¹ yan, kaau³ ngoh₂ ta² tsz₂.
一 个 西 人 教 我 打 字

9 How long have you been learning type writing ?
Nei₂ hok₄ ta² tsz, yau₂ kei² *noi₃ ni¹ ?
你 學 打 字 有 幾 耐 呢

10 About two months.
Sheung₃ *ha₃ leung₂ koh³ uet₄. 上 下 兩 个 月

11 Have you to buy typing ribbon ?
Ta² tsz, *taai³ shai² maai₂ m, shai² ?
打 字 帶 使 買 唔 使

12 I need not buy it there is some to use.
M, shai² maai² maai₂ yau₂ tak⁴ yung, a¹.
唔 使 買 有 得 用 吖

THE NINETEENTH LESSON

第 十 九 課—Tai₃ shap₁ kau² foh³

1	木	Muk₄—Wood.	6	眞	Chan¹—True.
2	張	Cheung¹—A sheet (Classifier).	7	熟	Shuk₄ — Ripe, wellvers-ed, cooked.
3	紙	Chi²—Paper.	8	牛	Ngau₁—Cow, cattle.
4	禮	Lai₂—Propriety, rites, conduct.	9	油	Yau₁—Oil, paint, butter.
5	拜	Paai³—Worship, Salute, (with lai₂ — Sunday)	10	燒	Shiu¹--Roast, burn.

1 呢件野係木做嘅. Ni¹ kin₂ ye₂ hai₂ muk₄ tso₂ ke³.

1 This is made of wood.

2 佢有幾張木檯. K'ui₂ yau₂ kei² cheung¹ muk₄ *t'oi₁.

2 He has several wooden tables.

3 你有銀紙冇. Nei₂ yau₂ ngan₁ chi² mo₂.

3 Have you any bank notes ?

4 舊時啲人好有禮. Kau shi₁ ti¹ yan₁ ho' yau₂ lai₂.

4 People formerly were very polite.

5 今日係禮拜一. Kam¹ yat₄ hai₂ lai₂ paai³ yat⁴.

5 To-day is Monday.

6 个个女人真係有錢. Koh² koh³ nui₂ *yan₁ chan¹ hai₃ yau₂ *ts'in₁.

6 That woman really has (a lot of) money.

7 呢啲肉生定熟呢. Ni¹ ti¹ yuk₄ shang¹ teng₃ (pe₃) shuk₄ ni¹ ?

7 Is this meat raw or cooked ?

8 我見一隻大水牛. Ngoh₂ kin'yat¹ chek₀ taai₃ shui² ngau₁.

8 I saw a large water buffalo.

9 你油乜野. Nei₂ yau₁ mat⁴ ye₂?

9 What are you painting ?

10 今日有燒牛肉冇？ Kam¹ yat₄ yau₂ shiu' ngau₁ yuk₁ mo₂ ?

10 Is there roast beef to-day

The Nineteenth Exercise—(Conversation.)

1 What day (of the week) is it to-day ?
Kam¹ yat₄ hai₃ lai₂ paai³ kei² ni¹ ?
今 日 係 禮 拜 幾 呢

2 To-day is Sunday.
Kam¹ yat₄ hai₃ lai₂ paai³. 今 日 係 禮 拜

3 What is there to eat on Sunday ?
Lai₂ paai³ yau₂ mat⁴ ye₂ shik₄ ?
禮 拜 有 乜 野 食

4 There is plenty to eat.
Yau₂ ho² toh¹ ye₂ shik₄. 有 好 多 野 食

5 I asked you what there was to eat ?
Ngoh₂ man₁ nei₂ yau₂ mat⁴ ye₂ shik₄ ?
我 問 你 有 乜 野 食

6 Look at the table and you will know.
Nei₂ t'ai² *t'oi₁ *min₃ tsau₃ chi¹.
你 睇 檯 面 就 知

7 Are there really so many things ?
Chan¹ hai₃ yau₂ kom² toh¹ ye₂ *ke² ?
眞 係 有 咁 多 野 嘅

8 Some people are coming to join us (at the meal).
Yau₂ yan₁ lai₁ shik₄ faan₃. 有 人 嚟 食 飯

9 What do you see on the table ?
Nei₂ kin³ *t'oi₁ *min₃ yau₂ mat⁴ ye₂ ?
你 見 檯 面 有 乜 野

10 I see lettuce and roast beef.
Ngoh₂ kin³ yau₂ shang¹ t'soi³, shiu¹ ngau₁ yuk₄.
我 見 有 生 菜, 燒 牛 肉

11 When are the people coming ?
Koh² ti¹ yan₁ kei² *shi₁ lai₁ ?
个 啲 人 幾 時 嚟

12 They will come directly (soon)
Tang² chan₃ tsau₃ lai₁. 等 陣 就 嚟

THE TWENTIETH LESSON

第 二 十 課—Tai₃ i₃ shap₄ foh³

1	遠	Uen₂—*Far, distant.*	6	窄	Chaak₀—*Narrow.*
2	近	Kan₃ (k'an₂)—*Near.*	7	左	Tsoh²—*Left.*
3	車	Ch'e¹—*Carriage, car*	8	右	Yau₃—*Right.*
4	坐	Ts'oh₂—*Sit.*	9	爛	Laan₃—*Broken, damaged.*
5	闊	Foot₀—*Wide.*	10	錯	Ts'oh³—*Error, mistake.*

1 去你處有幾遠呢. Hui³ nei₂ shue³ yau₂ kei² uen₂ ni¹ ?

1 How far is it to your place ?

2 冇幾遠好近. Mo₂ kei² uen₂ ho² k'an₂.

2 Not very far, it is very near.

3 佢有車冇. K'ui₂ yau₂ ch'e¹ mo₂ ?

3 Has he a carriage or not?

4 我出入要坐車. Ngoh₂ ch'ut⁴ yap₄ iu³ ts'oh₂ ch'e¹.

4 When I go about, I must go in a car (carriage).

5 呢間房好闊. Ni¹ kaan¹ *fong₁ ho² foot₀.

5 This room is very large (broad).

6 佢件衫尺寸窄. K'ui₂ kin₃ shaam¹ ch'ek₀ ts'uen⁸ chaak₀.

6 His coat is too narrow (in measurement).

7 个隻係左脚. Koh² chek₀ hai₃ tsoh² keuk₀.

7 That is the left leg.

8 你隻右手好番未呢. Nei₂ chek₀ yau₃ shau² ho² faan₁ mei₃ ni¹ ?

8 Is your right hand well yet ?

9 邊个打爛呢枝燈呢. Pin¹ koh³ ta² laan₃ ni¹ chi¹ tang¹ ni¹ ?

9 Who broke this lamp ?

10 佢講錯. K'ui₂ kong² ts'oh⁶.

10 He spoke wrongly (in error).

The Twentieth Exercise—(Conversation.)

1 Where are you going, that you must walk so quickly ?

Nei₂ hui³ pin¹ shue³ iu³ haang₁ tak⁴ kom³ faai⁸ ni¹ ?

你 去 邊 處 要 行 得 咁 快 呢

2 I have (some) business.

Ngoh₂ yau₂ sz₃. 我 有 事

3 If you want to be quick, why do you not ride ?

Seung² faai⁺ tim² kaai² m₁ ts'oh₂ ch'e¹ ni¹ ?

想 快 點 解 唔 坐 車 呢

4 It costs a lot of money to ride in a car.

Ts'oh₂ ch'e¹ iu³ ho² toh¹ *ngan₁.

坐 車 要 好 多 銀

5 How far are you going ?

Nei₂ hui⁺ kei² uen₂ ni¹ ? 你 去 幾 遠 呢

6 Not very far, it is rather near.

Mo₂ kei² uen₂, to¹ kei² k'an₂.

無 幾 遠, 都 幾 近

7 I think it is better to ride.

Ngoh₂ koo² ts'oh, ch'e¹ hui³ ho² ti¹.

我 估 坐 車 去 好 啲

8 Why is it better ?

Tim² kaai² ho² ti¹ ni¹ ? 點 解 好 啲 呢

9 First it is quicker, and second, it does not cost much.

Tai₁ yat⁴ kin₃ faai³ ti¹, tai₂ i₃ kin₃ m₁ shai² kei² toh¹ ngan₁. 第 一 件 快 啲, 第 二 件 唔 使 幾 多 銀

10 About how much money do you think ?

Nei₂ koo⁺ kei² toh¹ *ngan₁ kom³ sheung₃ *ha₃ ni¹ ?

你 估 幾 多 銀 咁 上 下 呢

11 I think about $ 1.50

Ngoh₂ koo² koh³ poon³ *ngan₁ *ts'iu₁ tsoh² *yau₃.

我 估 個 半 銀 錢 左 右

12 So then it is good.

Kom² to¹ ho². 咁 都 好

48

THE TWENTY FIRST LESSON

第 二 十 一 課—Tai₃ i₃ shap₄ yat⁴ foh³

1	貨	Foh°—Goods	6	美 Mei₂—Beautiful, America
2	貴	Kwai³—Dear, honourable	7	塊 Faai¹—A piece, slice (classifier)
3	計	Kai¹—To reckon, a plan	8	板 Paan²—A board, (of wood)
4	數	Sho°—Figures, numbers, accounts	9	高 Ko¹—High, noble, honourable
5	英	Ying¹—Brave, England	10	假 Ka²—False, ka,³ Holiday

1 我 想 買 啲 貨. Ngoh₂ seung² maai₂ ti¹ foh³.

1 I want to buy some goods.

2 銀 水 好 高. Ngan₁ shui² ho² ko¹.

2 The exchange is very dear (high).

3 你 計 乜 野 呢. Nei₂ kai³ mat⁴ ye₂ ni¹?

3 What are you reckoning?

4 我 計數. Ngoh₂ kai³ sho³.

4 I am reckoning accounts.

5 有 英 國 貨 到. Yau₂ ying¹ kwok₀ foh¹ to¹.

5 Some English goods have arrived.

6 佢 係 美 國 人 K'ui₂ hai₃ mei₂ kwok₀ yan .

6 He is an American.

7 呢 塊 係 乜 野. Ni¹ faai³ hai, mat⁴ ye₂?

7 What is this piece?

8 个 塊 係 木 板. Koh² faai³ hai₁ muk₄ paan².

8 That is a board (of wood).

9 係 唔 係 好 高. Hai₁ m₁ hai₃ ho² ko¹?

9 Is it very high?

10 唔 係, 係 假 貨. M₁ hai₃, hai₃ ka² foh³.

10 No, it is not the real article.

The Twenty First Exercise—(Conversation)

1 How wide is this board?

Ni^1 faai³ paan² yau₂ kei² foot₀ ni¹ ? 呢塊板有幾闊呢

2 That board is very narrow.

Koh² faai³ paan² ho² chaa₀k. 个塊板好窄.

3 How narrow is it?

Kei' chaak₀ ni¹? 幾窄呢.

4 I reckon it is about 8 inches.

Ngoh₂ kai² kwoh³ hai₃ paat₀ ts'uen³ kom³ sheung₃ *ha₃.
我 計 過 係 八 寸 咁 上 下

5 Is it really so narrow?

Chan¹ hai₃ kom³ chaak₀? 真 係 咁 窄

6 Do you think it is false, I do not tell lies.

Nei₂ koo² ka² ke⁹, ngoh₂ mo₂ kong² taai₃ wa₃ ke³.
你 估 假 嘅, 我 冇 講 大 話 嘅

7 So narrow, how much meney do you want for it ?

Kom³ chaak₀, iu⁵ kei² toh¹ *ngan₁ ni¹?
咁 窄, 要 幾 多 銀 呢.

8 Why is it so dear?

Tim² kaai² tak⁴ kom³ kwai³ ni¹?
點 解 得 咁 貴 呢.

9 You say it is very dear.

Nei₂ wa₃ ho² kwai³. 你 話 好 貴

10 Exchange (silver) is very high.

Ngan₁ shui² ho² ko¹. 銀 水 好 高.

11 Are the goods American or English?

Hai₃ mei₂ kwok₀ foh³ ting₃ (pe.) ying¹ kwok₀ foh⁸ ni¹ ?
係 美 國 貨 定 英 國 貨 呢

12 They are American.

Hai₃ mei₂ kwok₀ foh³. 係 美 國 貨.

' Often a sound like er is used in place of Ting₃

THE TWENTY SECOND LESSON

第 二 十 二 課—Tai₂ i₃ shap₁ i₃ foh³

1	倉	Ts'ong¹—*A godown, hold.*		
2	深	Sham¹—*Deep.*		
3	淺	Ts'in²—*Shallow.*		
4	內	Noi₃—*Inside.*		
5	物	Mat₄— *Articles, matter, material.*		
6	銅	T'ung₁—*Brass, copper.*		
7	分	Fan¹—*Divide, distinguish.* Fan³—*A share or portion.*		
8	重	Ch'ung₂—*Heavy,* chung₃ *besides, important.*		
9	實	Shat₄—*Solid, true, firm.*		
10	心	Sam¹—*Heart, mind.*		

1 呢間係貨倉. Ni¹ kaan¹ hai₃ foh³ ts'ong¹.

1 This is a godown.

2 貨倉有幾深呢. Foh⁵ ts'ong¹ yau₂ kei² sham¹ ni¹?

2 What is the depth of this godown?

3 冇幾深, 好淺. Mo₂ kei² sham¹, ho² ts'in².

3 Not very deep, it is very shallow.

4 倉內有乜野貨呢. Ts'ong¹ noi₃ yau₂ mat⁴ ye₂ foh³ ni¹?

4 What goods are in this godown?

5 有啲火水, 樣樣物件都有. Yau₂ ti¹ foh² shui², yeung₃*yeung₃ mat₄*kin₃ to¹ yau₂

5 There is some kerosene, and all kinds of things.

6 有銅冇呢? Yau₂ t'ung₁ mo₂ ni¹?

6 Is there any copper?

7 係分開擠唔係呢? Hai₃ fan¹ hoi¹ chai¹ m₁ hai₃ ni¹?

7 Are they stored separately?

8 銅重定鐵重呢? T'ung₁ ch'ung₂ ting₃ (pe₃) t'it₀ ch'ung₂ ni¹?

8 Is copper heavier or iron?

9 唔話得實. M₁ wa₃ tak⁴ shat₁.

9 I cannot say certainly (for certain).

10 有啲係實心嘅. Yau₂ ti¹ hai₃ shat₄ sam¹ ke³.

10 Some of it is solid.

The Twenty Second Exercise—(Conversation.)

1 Have you ordered goods ?
Nei₂ yau₂ †teng₂ foh³ mo₂ ? 你 有 定 貨 冇

2 The last few months I have not ordered any.
Ni¹ kei² koh³ uet₄ ngoh₂ mo₂ teng₂ foh°
呢 幾 个 月 我 冇 定 貨

3 Why do you not order ?
Tim² kaai² m₁ teng₅ ni¹ ? 點 解 唔 定 呢

4 I see that every thing is in a bad way.
Ngoh₂ kin° yeung₂ yeung₂ to¹ m₁ hai₂ ho². 我 見 樣 樣 都 唔 係 好

5 How much goods have you in the godown ?
Foh³ ts'ong¹ yau₂ kei² toh¹ foh³ ni¹ ? 貨 倉 有 幾 多 貨 呢

6 I still have a large quantity.
Chung₂ yau₂ l o² toh¹. 重 有 好 多

7 Do you want to order at once or not ?
Shai² kom° faai³ teng₂ m₁ shai² ? 使 咁 快 定 唔 使

8 I need not order so soon.
M₁ shai² teng₂ kom° faai³. 唔 使 定 咁 快

9 Copper and iron are not dear.
T'ung₁ t'it₀ m₁ hai₅ kwai°. 銅 鐵 唔 係 貴

10 I know they are not dear, but I have no money to buy them.
Ngoh₂ chi¹ m₁ hai₂ kwai°, taan₅ ngoh₂ mo₂ *ts'in₁ maai₂. 我 知 唔 係 貴, 但 我 冇 錢 買

11 If you have no money, you can pay in instalments.
Nei₂ mo₂ *ts'in,₁ fan¹ hoi¹ pei² to¹ tak⁴. 你 冇 錢 分 開 俾 都 得

12 I must consider the matter even if I may pay in instalments
Fan¹ hoi¹ pei² ngoh₂ to¹ iu³ seung² kwoh³ chi° tak⁴
分 開 俾 我 都 要 想 過 至 得

† Teng   A longer sound.

THE TWENTY THIRD LESSON

第 二 十 三 課—Tai i, 'bap, saam¹ foh³

1	便 P'in₃—Convenient, side	6	補 Po²—To repair.
2	紅 Hung₁—Red.	7	爐 Lo₁—A boiler.
3	藍 Laam₁—Blue.	8	聞 Man₁—To hear.
4	旗 K'ei₁—A flag.	9	掃 So³—To sweep, a broom.
5	椅 I'—A chair.	10	釘 Teng¹—A nail.

1 我左手便屋有个西人. Ngoh₂ tsoh² shau² pin₃ uk⁴ yau₂ koh³ sai¹ yan.

1 There is a westerner in the house at my left.

2 佢嘅面係紅色. K'ui₂ ke³ min₃ hai₃ hung₁ shik⁴

2 His face is red.

3 呢張紙係藍色. Ni¹ cheung¹ chi² hai₃ laam₁ shik⁴.

3 This paper is blue.

4 呢枝係半白半紅旗. Ni¹ chi¹ hai₃ poon³ paak₄ poon³ hung₁ k'ei₁.

4 This flag is half white and half red.

5 个張係四方椅. Koh³ cheung¹ hai₃ sz' tong¹ i².

5 That is a square chair.

6 佢補衫. K'ui₂ po³ shaam¹

6 He repairs clothes (coats)

7 我做補爐. Ngoh₂ tso po² lo₁.

7 I repair boilers.

8 你聞得人講係唔係. Nei₂ man₁ tak⁴ yan₁ kong² hai₃ m₁ hai₁?

8 Did you hear some one say it?

9 快啲掃乾淨啲地方. Faai' ti¹ so' kon¹ tseng₃ ti¹ tei₃ fong.

9 Quickly sweep the place clean.

10 俾一口釘我. Pei' yat⁴ hau² teng¹ ngoh₂.

10 Give me a nail

The Twenty Third Exercise—(Conversation.)

1 What is the weather like to day ?
Kam[1] yat[4] t'in[1] shi[1] tim[2] *yeung[5] ni[1] ?
今 日 天 時 點 樣 呢

2 It is very cold to day.
Kam[1] yat[4] ho[2] laang[2].　今 日 好 冷

3 What can we do as it is cold ?
Kom[3] laang[2] ngoh[2] iu[3] tim[2] *yeung[3] ni[1] ?
咁 冷 我 要 點 樣 呢

4 As we have a stove we need not fear.
Yau[2] foh[2] lo[1] m[1] p'a[3].　有 火 爐 唔 怕

5 You must (sweep) clean your stove.
Nei[2] koh[3] foh[2] lo[1] iu[3] so[5] kwoh[3] chi[3] ta[5].
你 个 火 爐 要 掃 過 至 得

6 I will call a servant to clean it soon.
Ngoh[2] yat[4] *chan[3] tsau[3] kiu[3] koh[3] kung[1] yan[1] so[3].
我 一 陣 就 叫 个 工 人 掃

7 What is that on the mantelpiece ?
Foh[2] lo[1] t'au[1] koh[2] ti[1] hai[3] mat[4] ye[2] ?
火 爐 頭 个 啲 係 乜 野

8 Those things on the mantelpiece are newspapers.
Foh[2] lo[1] t'au[1] koh[2] kei[2] cheung[1] hai[3] san[1] man[1] chi[2].
火 爐 頭 个 幾 張 係 新 聞 紙

9 Bring a chair for me.
Ning[1] cheung[1] i[2] lai[1] ngoh[2].　搛 張 椅 嚟 我

10 What do you want a chair for ?
Nei[2] in[3] i[2] lai[1] tso[3] mat[4] ye[2] ?
你 要 椅 嚟 做 乜 野

11 I want a chair to sit on, and see (read) the newspapers ?
Ngoh[2] iu[3] i[2] lai[1] ts'oh[2], hai[2] shue[3] t'ai[2] san[1] man[1] chi[2].
我 要 椅 嚟 坐 喺 處 睇 新 聞 紙

12 There was a lot of news in yesterday's paper.
Tsok[4] yat[4] san[1] man[1] chi[2] yan[2] ho[4] toh[1] ye[2] maai[3].
昨 日 新 聞 紙 有 好 多 野 賣

THE TWENTY FOURTH LESSON

第 二 十 四 課—Tai₃ i₃ shap₄ sz³ foh³

1	變	Pin³—*Change.*	6	老	Lo₂—*Old, aged.*
2	凍	Tung²—*Cold.*	7	請	Ts'ing²—*Request, invite.*
3	暖	Nuen₂—*Warm.*	8	東	Tung¹—*East.*
4	布	Po³—*Cloth, spread out.*	9	南	Naam₁—*South.*
5	搵	Wan²—*Seek, find.*	10	北	Pak⁴—*North.*

1 你件衫變色 Nei₂ kin₂ shaam¹ pin³ shik⁴

1 Your coat has changed in colour.

2 凍水洗身好凍 Tung³ shui² sai² shan¹ ho² tung³.

2 It is very cold to wash in cold water.

3 今日暖番啲 Kam¹ yat₄ nuen₂ faan¹ ti¹.

3 It is warmer again to-day.

4 我要買啲布嚟做衫 Ngoh₂ iu³ maai₂ ti¹ po³ lai₁ tso shaam¹.

4 I must buy some cloth to make a coat.

5 有人搵你 Yau₂ yan₁ wan² nei₂.

5 Some one is looking for you.

6 佢有幾老呢 K'ui₂ yau₂ kei² lo₂ ni¹?

6 How old is he?

7 昨日有人請我飲茶 Tsok₄ yat₄ yau₂ yan₁ ts'ing² ngoh₂ yam² ch'a₁.

7 Yesterday a person invited me to (drink) tea.

8 遠東有好多國 Uen₂ tung¹ yau₂ ho² toh¹ kwok₀

8 In the Far East there are many countries.

9 南方都幾熱 Naam₁ fong¹ to¹ kei² it₁.

9 The south is fairly hot.

10 你去過英國北便未呢 Nei₂ hui³ kwoh³ ying¹ kwok₀ pak⁴**pin₃ mei₃ ni¹?

10 Have you been to the North of England yet?

The Twenty Fourth Exercise—(Conversation.)

1 The weather is always changing.

T'in¹ shik⁴ shi₁ shi₁ pin³. 天 色 時 時 變

2 Yes, it is uncertain.

Hai-, mo₂ teng₃ ke³. 係, 冇 定 嘅.

3 The South and North are different.

Naam₁ fong¹ Pak⁴ fong¹ hai, m₁ t'ung₁.

南 方 北 方 係 唔 同.

4 How are they different?

Yau₂ mat⁴ m₁ t'ung₁ ni¹? 有 乜 唔 同 呢.

5 They are different in temperature, (hot and cold)

Yat⁴ laang₂ yat⁴ it₄ tsau₁ m₁ t'ung₁.

一 冷 一 熱 就 唔 同

6 I fear the cold very much.

Ngoh₂ ho² p'a³ laang₂ ke³. 我 好 怕 冷 嘅

7 How can you fear as you have so money clothes?

Nei₂ yau₂ kom¹ toh¹ shaam¹, p'a³ mat⁴ ye₂ ni¹? 你 有 咁 多 衫 怕 乜 野 呢.

8 Having so many clothes is not convenient.

Yau₂ shaam¹ to¹ m₁ fong¹ pin, ke⁴.

有 衫 都 唔 方 便 嘅.

9 How is it inconvenient ?

Yau₂ mat⁴ ye₂ m₁ fong¹ pin₁ ni ?

有 乜 野 唔 方 便 呢.

10 To speak of nothing else, it is not convenient for going about (in and out).

Ch'ut⁴ yap₄ tsau₁ m₁ fong¹ pin₃, m₁ shai³ kong² tai₂ i₃ *yeung₃. 出 入 就 唔 方 便, 唔 使 講 第 二 樣

11 It is better to live in the tropics.

Chue₂ it₄ taai³ tei₂ fong¹ ho¹ ti¹ ke⁴.

住 熱 帶 地 方 好 的 嘅.

12 That is certainly so.

Yat⁴ ting, hai₃. 一 定 係.

THE TWENTY-FIFTH LESSON

第 二 十 五 課—Tai, i, shap, ng₂ foh³

1	盤	P'oon₁—*A dish, a classifier, examine.*
2	算	Suen³—*Reckon, regard, estimate.*
3	部	Po₃—*Classifier for book, a department.*
4	唐	T'ong₁—*Chinese, name of dynasty.*
5	作	Tsok₀ — *Make, do, be, regard as.*
6	文	Man₁—*Literature, composition, literary style*
7	章	Cheung¹ — *A chapter, (man₁ cheung¹) essay.*
8	程	Ch'ing₁—*A route, (cheung¹ ch'ing₁), scheme, regulation.*
9	墨	Mak₄—*Ink.*
10	咗	Choh² (Jaw²) — *Finish, past tense.*

1 呢个面盤幾好. Ni' koh³ min₃ *p'oon₁ kei² ho². — This wash basin is rather good.

2 我想學算數. Ngoh₂ seung² hok₄ suen³ sho³. — I want to learn arithmetic.

3 我買三部書嚟學. Ngoh₂ maai₂ saam¹ po₃ shue¹ lai₁ hok₄. — I am buying three books to learn (from).

4 係買唐書唔係呢. Hai, maai₂ t'ong₁ shue¹ m₁ hai₃ ni¹? — Are you buying Chinese books?

5 好多人作書教人. Ho² toh¹ yan₁ tsok₀ shue¹ kaau³ yan₁. — Many people make books to teach.

6 我買書嚟學作文. Ngoh₂ maai₂ shue¹ lai₁ hok₄ tsok₀ man₁. — I am buying books to learn to write composition.

7 呢章係乜野書呢. Ni¹ cheung¹ hai₃ mat⁴ ye₂ shue¹ ni¹? — What is this chapter?

8 个章係教人學唐話嘅章程. Koh² cheung¹ hai₃ kaau³ yan₁ hok₄ t'ong₁ *wa₃ ke³ cheung¹ ch'ing₁. — That chapter is a method for teaching people to speak Chinese.

9 你有買墨水筆冇? Nei₂ yau₂ maai₂ mak₄ shui² pat⁴ mo₂? — Have you bought a pen?

10 有,墨水筆咁有用,我買咗好耐. Yau₂, mak₄ shui² pat⁴ kom³ yau₂ yung₃, ngoh₂ maai₂ choh² ho² noi₃ (lo³). — Yes, a pen is so useful, and I bought one a long time ago.

The Twenty-fifth Exercise—(Conversation.)

1 Sir, please teach me to read.

Sin¹ shaang¹ ts'ing² nei₂ kaau³ ngoh₂ tuk₄ shue¹.

先 生 請 你 教 我 讀 書

2 What books do you want to read ?

Nei₂ seung² tuk₄ mat⁴ ye₂ shue¹ ?

你 想 讀 乜 野 書

3 I want to read Chinese books and write Chinese characters

Ngoh₂ seung² tuk₄ t'ong₁ shue¹ se² t'ong₁ tsz₃.

我 想 讀 唐 書 寫 唐 字

4 Have you bought books yet ?

Yau₂ maai₂ to² shue¹ mei₃ ni¹ ?　有 買 倒 書 未 呢

5 Please buy three books for me.

Ts'ing² sin¹ shaang¹ t'ung₁ ngoh, maai₂ saam¹ po₃.

請 先 生 同 我 買 三 部

6 In writing Chinese words one must learn Chinese Composition.

Se² t'ong₁ tsz₃ iu³ hok₄ tsok₀ t'ong₁ man₁.

寫 唐 字 要 學 作 唐 文

7 Some say one must learn to write essays.

Yau₂ yan₁ wa, iu³ hok₄ tsok₀ man₁ cheung¹.

有 人 話 要 學 作 文 章

8 One must work hard to learn essay writing.

Seung² hok₄ tsok₀ man₁ cheung¹ iu³ ho² yung₃ sam¹ chi³ tak⁴

想 學 作 文 章 要 好 用 心 至 得

9 Have you learnt arithmetic yet ?

Nei₂ hok₄ suen³ sho³ mei₃ ni¹ ?　你 學 算 數 未 呢

10 I want to buy an abacus to learn.

Ngoh₂ seung² maai₂ suen³ p'oon₁ lai₁ hok₄.

我 想 買 算 盤 嚟 學

11 You can use pen and ink to reckon with.

Yung₃ pat⁴ mak₄ kai³ sho³ to¹ tak⁴ (lo³).

用 筆 墨 計 數 都 得

THE TWENTY SIXTH LESSON

第 二 十 六 課—Tai$_5$ i$_3$ shap$_4$ luk$_4$ foh^5.

1	親	Ts'an^1— *Near, relations, self.*		6	姊	Tsz^2—*Elder sister.*
2	父	Foo$_3$—*Father.*		7	妹	Mooi$_3$—*Younger sister.*
3	母	Mo$_2$—*Mother.*		8	友	Yau$_2$—*Friend.*
4	兄	Hing^1—*Elder brother.*		9	朋	P'ang$_1$—*Friend, (used with yau)*
5	弟	Tai$_2$—*Younger brother.*		10	佬	Lo^2—*A person, fellow*

1 我親身去見佢 Ngoh$_2$ ts'an^1 shan^1 hui^3 kin^3 k'ui$_2$.

1 I went myself (in person) to see him.

2 我父親喺屋†企做工 Ngoh$_2$ foo$_3$ ts'an^1 hai^2 uk^4 k'ei^2 tso$_3$ kung^1.

2 My father is at home working.

3 佢母親就嚟見佢 K'ui$_2$ mo$_2$ ts'an^1 tsau$_3$ lai$_1$ kin^3 k'ui$_2$.

3 His mother is coming soon to see him.

4 家兄唔喺屋企 Ka^1 hing^1 m$_1$ hai^2 uk^4 k'ei^2.

4 (My) elder brother is not at home.

5 我有四兄弟,一个大,兩个細同我係四兄弟 Ngoh$_2$ yau$_2$ sz^3 hing^1 tai$_2$, yat^4 koh^3 taai$_3$, leung$_2$ koh^3 sai^c t'ung$_1$ ngoh$_2$ hai$_2$ sz^3 hing^i tai$_2$.

5 I have four brothers, one elder brother, two younger brothers and myself, being four brothers.

6 你大姊去邊處呢 Nei$_2$ taai$_3$ tsz^2 hui^3 pin^1 shue^3 ni^1?

6 Where has your elder sister gone?

7 佢同我个妹去上海. K'ui$_2$ t'ung$_1$ ngoh$_2$ koh^3 *mooi$_3$ hui^3 sheung$_3$ hoi^2.

7 She has gone to Shanghai with my younger-sister.

8 我有好多書友 Ngoh$_2$ yau$_2$ ho^2 toh^1 shue^1 *yau$_2$.

8 I have many school fellows.

9 佢有三个朋友 K'ui$_2$ yau$_2$ saam^1 koh^3 p'ang$_1$ yau$_2$.

9 He has three friends.

10 打鐵工人叫做打鐵佬 Ta^2 t'it$_0$ kung^1 yan$_1$ kiu^3 tso$_3$ ta^2 t'it$_0$ lo^2.

10 Workers in iron, are called iron worker fellows

†Note 唫 K'ei^2 is more frequently used for family or home.

The Twenty Sixth Exercise—(Conversation.)

1 Sir, I wish to go home for a few days.
   Sin¹ shaang¹, ngoh₂ seung² faan¹ uk⁴ ke'i² kei² yat₄
   先生，我想番屋企幾日

2 Why do you want to go home?
   Tso₃ mat⁴ iu³ faan¹ uk⁴ k'ei² ni¹?
   做乜婺番屋企呢

3 My parents tell me to go.
   Ngoh₃ foo₃ mo₂ kiu⁻ ngoh₂ hui⁵
   我父母叫我去

4 What is the matter?
   Yau₂ mat⁴ ye₂ sz₃ ni¹?   有乜野事呢.

5 My mother has some business.
   Ngoh₃ mo₂ ts'an¹ yau₃ ti¹ sz₃   我母親有啲事.

6 Is it your brothers' affairs?
   Hai₃ m₁ hai₃ nei₂ hing¹ tai₃ ke⁵ sz₃ ni¹?
   係唔係你兄弟嘅事呢

7 I do not know.   My mother is not very well.
   Ngoh₂ m₁ chi¹ a¹,   ngoh₂ lo₂ *mo₂ m₁ hai₅ kei² ho².
   我唔知呀，我老母唔係幾好

8 Why do your sisters not attend to her?
   Tso₃ mat⁴ nei, tsz² *mooi₃ m₁ pei² ye₂ k'ui₂ shik₄ ni¹?
   做乜你姊妹唔俾野佢食呢.

9 My sisters are young.
   Ngoh₂ tsz² *mooi₃ sai³ koh³.   我姊妹細个.

10 Why must (want) you go?
   Tim² kaai² iu⁸ nei₂ hui⁵ ni¹?   點解要你去呢.

11 My mother has a cold and fever.
   Ngoh₂ lo₂ *mo₂ laang₂ ts'an¹, shan¹ it₄   我老母冷親身熱.

12 Well, you must come back quickly.
   Ho² a³, nei₂ iu³ faai⁵ ti¹ faan¹ lai₃
   好呀，你要快啲番嚟

THE TWENTY-SEVENTH LESSON

第 二 十 七 課—Tai₃ i₃ shap₄ ts'at⁴ foh³

1	每	Mooi₂—*Each, every.*	6	即	Tsik⁴—*At once, immediately.*
2	歲	Sui³—*Year, (of age).*	7	刻	Hak⁴—*Cut, carve, moment.*
3	添	T'im¹—*Increase, further, add.*	8	晏	Aan³—*Late, noon.*
4	晨	Shan₁—*Period, morning.*	9	期	K'ei₁—*Date, fixed time.*
5	初	Ch'oh¹—*Beginning, first.*	10	滿	Moon₂—*Full.*

1 你每日幾點鐘起身呢.
Nei₂ mooi₂ yat₄ kei² tim² chung¹ hei² shan¹ ni¹ ?

2 年年起頭,人人加一歲.
Nin₁ Nin₁ hei²*t'au₁, yan₁ yan₁ ka¹ yat⁴ sui³.

3 你咁講就添一歲. Nei₂ kom⁴ kong² tsau₃ t'im¹ yat⁴ sui³.

4 朝早見人,就話早晨.
Chiu¹ tso⁴ kin³ yan₁, tsau₃ wa₃ tso² shan₁.

5 初初起身你做乜野呢.
Ch'oh¹ ch'oh¹ hei² shan¹ nei₂ tso₃ mat⁴ ye₂ ni¹ ?

6 初初起身係即時讀書唔係. Ch'oh¹ ch'oh¹ hei² shan¹ hai₃ tsik⁴ shi₁ tuk₄ shue¹ m₁ hai₃.

7 唔係即刻讀書,係洗面先. M₁ hai₃ tsik⁴ hak⁴ tuk₄ shue¹, hai₃ sai² min₃ sin¹.

8 你讀書讀到好晏. Nei₂ tuk₄ shue¹ tuk₄ to³ ho² aan³.

9 一年有幾多个學期呢.
Yat⁴ nin₁ yau₂ kei² toh¹ koh³ hok₄ k'ei₁ ni¹ ?

10 有三个學期, 呢个學期就滿. Yau₂ saam¹ koh³ hok₄ k'ei₁, ni¹ koh³ hok₄ k'ei₁ tsau₃ moon₂.

1 What time do you get up every day ?

2 At the beginning of each year, every one adds one year to his age.

3 When you say that, you mean that they add a year to their age.

4 When you see people early, you say "Good morning" (early time).

5 When you first get up what do you do ?

6 When you get up do you read immediately ?

7 No, I do not read at once, I wash my face first.

8 Do you read till late in the morning ?

9 How many terms are there in the (school).

10 There are three terms. This term is nearly ended (full).

61

The Twenty-seventh Exercise—(Conversation.)

1 Good morning, have you had your breakfast (rice) yet ?

Tso² shan₁, shik₄ faan₃ mei₃ ni¹?　早晨,食飯未呢.

2 Not yet, have you eaten yet?

Mei₃ a¹, nei₂ shik₄ choh² mei₃ ni¹?
未吔, 你食嘅未呢.

3 I have eaten. What time do you breakfast every morning?

Shik₄ choh² lok₀, nei₂ mooi₂ chiu¹ kei² tim² chung¹ shik₄ faan₃ ni¹?　食嘅咯,你每朝幾點鐘食飯呢.

4 We eat very late (in the morning)?

Ngoh₂ tei₃ ho² aan³ shik₄ faan₃ ke'.
我 地 好 晏 食 飯 嘅 .

5 Why you are so late?

Tim² kaai² kom³ aan³ ni¹?　點解咁晏呢.

6 We are always so.

Ngoh₂ tei₃ shi₁ shi₁ to¹ hai₃ kom².
我 地 時 時 都 係 咁 .

7 Do you think (say) it is good to eat so late?

Nei₂ wa₃ kom³ aan³ shik₄ faan₃ ho² m₁ ho² ni¹?
你 話 咁 晏 食 飯 好 唔 好 呢 .

8 Chinese are so, Westerners are about the same.

T'ong₁ yan₁ hai₃ kom², Sai¹ yan₁ to¹ hai₃ kom² sheung₃*ha₃.
唐 人 係 咁, 西 人 都 係 咁 上 下 .

9 Do they live to be as old as Westerners?

M₁ chi¹ k'ui₃ tei₃ nin₁ sui³ yau₂ sai¹ yan₁ kom³ toh¹ mo₂ ni¹?　唔知佢地年歲有西人咁多冇呢.

10 Some Chinese say that there are very few old Europeans.

Yau₂ ti¹ t'ong₁ yan₁ wa₃, sai¹ yan₁ ho² shiu² yau₂ lo₂ yan₁.
有 啲 唐 人 話 西 人 好 少 有 老 人 .

11 I see some old Chinese, but not many.

Ngoh₂ kin³ yau₂ ti¹ t'ong₁ yan₁ hai₃ lo₂, taan₃ hai₃ mo₂ kom³ toh¹.　我見有啲唐人係老,但係冇咁多.

12 Young Chinese are numerous.

Hau₃ shaang¹ ke³ t'ong₁ yan₁ hai₃ toh¹.
後 生 嘅 唐 人 係 多

THE TWENTY-EIGHTH LESSON

第 二 十 八 課—Tai₃ i₃ shap₄ paat₀ foh³

1	肥	Fei₁—*Fat.*	6	硬	Ngaang₋—*Hard (substance).*
2	瘦	Shau³, sau³—*Thin, lean.*	7	厚	Hau₂—*Thick* Hau₋—*Virtuous*
3	難	Naan₁—*Hard, difficult.* Naan₃—*Difficulties.*	8	薄	Pok₄—*Thin.*
4	易	I₋ — *Easy,* yik₄, *to exchange, barter (deal with)*	9	河	Hoh₁—*River.*
5	音	Yam¹— *Sound, voice.*	10	運	Wan₃ — *Movement, remove, transport.*

1 个隻牛係肥唔係. Koh² cheko ngau₁ hai₃ fei₁ m₁ hai₃ ?

1 Is that cow fat or not ?

2 唔係, 个隻牛係好瘦. M₁ hai₃, koh² cheko ngau₁ hai₃ ho² shau³.

2 No, that cow is very thin.

3 學唐話係唔係難呢. Hok₄ t'ong₁ *wa₃ hai₃ m₁ hai₃ naan₁ ni¹ ?

3 Is it difficult to learn Chinese or not ?

4 唔係幾難用心學就易. M₁ hai₃ kei² naan₁ yung₃ sam¹ hok₄ tsau₃ i₃.

4 Not very difficult, if you use your mind it is easy.

5 講唐話娿好口音至講得好. Kong² t'ong₁ *wa₃ iu³ ho² hau² yam¹ chi kong² tak⁴ ho².

5 In speaking Chinese one must have good enunciation to be able to speak well.

6 唔好食硬野. M₁ ho² shik₄ ngaang₃ ye₀.

6 Do not eat hard things.

7 天熱娿厚衫唔娿呢. T'in¹ it₄ iu³ hau₂ shaam¹ m₁ iu³ ni¹ ?

7 Do you need a thick coat in hot weather.

8 唔娿, 天熱我要薄衫, 天冷至娿厚衫. M₁ iu³, t'in¹ it₄ ngoh₃ iu³ pok₄ shaam¹, t'in¹ laang₂ chi³ iu³ hau₂ shaam¹.

8 No, in hot weather I need thin clothes, only in cold weather I need thick clothes.

9 河水多數係淺嘅. Hoh₁ shui² toh¹ sho³ hai₃ ts'in² ke⁵.

9 Rivers are mostly shallow.

10 中國有條運河. Chung¹ kwok₀ yau₂ t'iu₁ wan₃ hoh₁.

10 There is a Canal in China.

The Twenty-eighth Exercise—(Conversation.)

1 Good morning, are you well to-day?

Kom³ tso² shan₁, kam¹ yat₄ ho² a¹? 咁早晨,今日好吖.

2 Yes, thanks, (I hope) you are well?

Ho²aᵉ, yau₂ sam₁, sin¹ shaang¹ ho²? 好呀,有心,先生好.

3 Thank you. To-day we will go for a walk in the street and talk as we go.

Yau₂ sam,¹ kam¹ yat₄ t'ung₁ neiz hui³ kaai¹, ngob₂ tei: yat⁴ lo₃ haang₁ yat⁴ lo₅ kong² 有心,今日同你去街,我哋一路行一路講.

4 Good, what shall we talk about?

Ho² a¹, kong² mat⁴ ye₂ ho² ni¹? 好吖,講乜野好呢.

5 Shall we talk about men (good or not)?

Kong² yan₁ ho² m₁ ho² ni¹? 講人好唔好呢.

6 Good, what is it good to say about men?

Ho², yan₁ yau₂ mat⁴ ye₂ ho² kong² ni¹? 好,人有乜野好講呢.

7 A few days ago we talked about food. to-day we will talk about man's body.

Sin¹ kei² yat₄ kong² shik₄, kam¹ yat₄ kong² yan₁ ke³ shan¹. 先幾日講食,今日講人嘅身.

8 Is it better to eat much or little?

Shik₄ toh¹ ho² teng₃ shik₄ shiu² ho² ni¹? 食多好定食少好呢.

9 If you eat more you are fatter; if you eat less you are thinner; is that so?

Shik₄ toh¹ ti¹ fei₁ ti¹, shik₄ shiu² ti¹ shau³ ti¹'; hai₃ m₁ hai₅ ni¹? 食多啲肥啲,食少啲瘦啲;係唔係呢.

10 Some people eat a great deal but they are thin. Some eat very little yet they are very fat.

Yau₂ ti¹ yan¹ shik₄ ho² toh¹, taan₃ hai₃ ho² shau³, yau₂ ti¹ yan₁ shik₄ ho² shiu², taan₃ hai₅ ho² fei₁. 有啲人食好多,但係好瘦,有的人食好少,但係好肥.

11 So, each of them is different. some eat and are not well.

Kom²keᵉ, kok₀ yau₂ kok₀ m₁ t'ung₁, yau₂ ti¹ yan₁ shik₄ to¹ m₁ tak⁴ ho². 咁嘅,各有各唔同,有啲人食都唔得好.

12 Why are they not well if they have food?

Tim² kaai² yau₂ tak⁴ shik₄ to¹ m₁ ho² ni¹? 點解有得食都唔好呢.

13 It is well for one to be careful in food and drink.

Yan₁ yan₁ shik₄ chan¹ hai₃ iu³ siu² sam¹ chi³ ho². 人人食真係要小心至好.

A SHORT LIST OF CLASSIFIERS OR NUMERATIVES.

1. 个 koh³ used for men, and generally.
2. 隻 chek₀ used for animals, birds, boats, **some** parts of body.
3. 件 kin₃ used for matters of business, **objects,** coats.
4. 間 kaan¹ used for houses, buildings, **rooms.**
5. 條 t'iu₁ used for many long things, **road,** chain, fish, trousers.
6. 張 cheung¹ used for tables, chairs, **sheets of** paper, beds, carpets, knives, etc.
7. 塊 faai³ used for slices of bread, **pieces of** cloth, wood, paper.
8. 幅 fuk⁴ used for maps, pictures, walls, **pieces** of ground.
9. 封 fung¹ used for letters.
10. 口 hau² used for nails, pistols, men.
11. 駕 ka³ used for carriages, cars.
12. 枝 chi¹ used for pens, pencils, masts, branches, flags.
13. 場 ch'eung₁ used for battles, law cases, matters, business.
14. 文 *man₁ used for money, cash.
15. 粒 nap² used for grains, rice, sand, pills.
16. 部 po₃ used for books.
17. 把 pa² used for fans, umbrellas, knives, **and** articles that may be held.
18. 位 *wai₂ used for people.
19. 笪 taat₀ used for places, land.
20. 頂 ting² used for hats, sedan chairs.
21. 度 to₂ used for bridges, doors, rivers, etc.
22. 對 tui⁸ used for pairs of things, **shoes,** scrolls, etc.
23. 陣 chan₃ used for time, wind, showers, flashes.

英粵通語 Cantonese for everyone ——香港大學粵語教材（一九三一）

A SHORT LIST OF FINALS.

The characters used for these are mostly made up for the purpose.

1.	呀	A^1	euphonic, is used in two different tones.
2.	吖	a^1	emphatic.
3.	啫 or 喳	{che^1 or cha^1}	in different tones, implies limitation, used for only.
4.	嘅	ke'	euphonic.
5.		kwa^3	implies doubt, probably, used in two tones.
6.	喇	la^1	emphatic, sometimes imperative.
7.	哩	le^1	used in various tones, mostly euphonic, sometimes emphatic.
8.	咯	lok_5	(k) usually silent like loh^3 euphonic.
9.	嗎	ma^3	used in six tones, interrogative.
10.	咩	me^1	interrogative.
11.	麽	moh^1	used in six tones, interrogative.
12.	嗱	na_1	emphatic.
13.	嚀	ne^1	used in five tones, emphatic.
14.	呢	ni^1	interrogative.
15.	噃	poh^3	emphatic, used after loh^3.
16.	啝	woh_3	in three tones or wa in three tones, a quotation.

English	Chinese	Romanization
again (further)	又	yau_3, 亦 yik_4, 再 $tsoi^3$
all	喊嘭呤	$haam_3$ $pa(ng)_3$ $laang_3$
all round (all directions)	週 圍	$chau^1$ wai_1
although	雖 然	sui^1 in_1
always	時 時	shi_1 shi_1, 常時 $sheung_1$ shi_1
because	因 爲	yan^1 wai_3
besides, further	而 且	i_1 $ch'e^2$, 又 yau_3
blessing	福	fuk^4
boundary (class)	界	$kaai^3$, (student class) 學界 $hok_4 kaai^3$
butterflies	蝴 蝶	oo_1 *tip_4
cannot be helped	冇柰何	mo_2 noi_3 hoh_1
cannot help	柰晤何	noi_3 m_1 hoh_1
club	俱樂部	$k'ui^1$ lok_4 po_3 (H.K. Club)
	新公司	san^1 $kung^1$ sz^1
command, order	吩 咐	fan^1 foo^3
common, general	平 常	$p'eng_1$ $sheung_1$
company	公 司	$kung^1$ sz^1
complete, perfect	完 全	uen_1 $ts'uen_1$
customs, manners	規 矩	$kw'ai^1$ kui^2, 風俗 $fung^1$ $tsuk_4$
descendants	子 孫	tsz^2 $suen^1$
discuss	斟 酌	$cham^1$ $cheuk_0$
domestic animals	畜 牲	$ch'uk^4$ $shang^1$
effect, influence	影 响	$ying^2$ $heung^2$
establish set up, begin	設 立	$ch'it_0$ $laap_4$
examination	考 試	$haau^2$ shi^3
examine	查 察	$ch'a_1$ $ch'aat_0$
family	家 人	ka^1 yan_1
fragments (small)	零 碎	$leng_1$, sui^3
frequently	時 常	shi_1 $sheung_1$
glass	玻 璃	poh^1 *lei_1
God	上 帝	$sheung_3$ tai^3
good morning	早 晨	tso^2 $shan_1$
good order, in	安 當	$t'oh_2$ $tong^3$

government	國家	kwok$_0$ ka^1, 政府 ching^3 foo^2
if	如果	ue$_1$ kwoh^2, 倘若 t'ong^2 yeuk$_4$
influence	感動	kom^2 tung$_3$
Jesus	耶穌	ye$_1$ so^1
king	皇帝	wong$_1$ tai^3
like (seems)	似乎	ts'z$_2$ oo$_1$ (foo$_1$)
material	材料	ts'oi$_1$ liu$_3$
moment	一陣	yat^4 chan$_3$
movement	運動	wan$_3$ tung$_3$
myriad (10,000)	一萬	yat^4 maan$_3$
needlework	針黹	cham^1 chi^2
neighbour	隔籬	kaak$_0$ lei$_1$
occasionally	內中	noi$_2$ chung^1, 耐不耐 noi$_3$ pat^4 *noi$_3$
originally	本來	poon^2 loi$_1$, 原本 uen$_1$ poon^2
or	嘅	pe$_3$, 或 waak$_4$, 定 ting$_2$, 呀 a$_3$ 嗎 me$_3$
peaceful	安樂	on^1 lok$_4$, 和平 woh$_1$ p'eng$_1$
perfect	完全	uen$_1$ ts'uen$_1$
perhaps	或者	waak$_4$ che^2
police station	差館	ch'aai^1 koon^2, 警局 king^2 *kuk$_4$
politics	政治	ching^3 chi$_3$
prepare	預備	ue$_3$ pei$_3$
reason, a	緣故	uen$_1$ koo^3, 原因 uen$_1$ yan^1
regard as	以爲	i$_2$ wai$_1$
sacrifice (self)	犧牲	hei^1 shang^1
school	學校	hok$_4$ haau$_3$, 書館 shue^1 koon^2
self	自己	tsz$_3$ kei^2
sing songs	唱歌	ch'eung^3 koh^1
students	學生	hok$_4$ shang^1
study	研究	in$_1$ kau^3, 學 hok$_4$
therefore	所以	shoh^2 i$_2$
universal (general)	普通	p'o^2 t'ung^1
we, this and that	彼此	pei^2 ts'z^2

THE TWENTY NINTH LESSON

第 二 十 九 課—Tai₃ i₃ shap₄ kau² foh³

1	肚	T'o₂—Stomach.	6	耳	I₂—Ear, Ears.
2	餓	Ngoh₃—Hungry.	7	牙	Nga₁—Tooth, teeth.
3	眼	Ngaan₂—Eyes	8	指	Chi²—Fingers, refer to, point.
4	瞓	Fan³—Sleep.	9	自	Tsz₃—From, self.
5	痛	T'ung⁷—Painful.	10	己	Kei²—Self.

1 我食野落肚 Ngoh₂ shik₄ ye₂ lok₄ t'o₂.

1 My food goes into my stomach.

2 食咗野肚唔餓 Shik₄ choh² ye₂ t'o₂ m₁ ngoh₃.

2 After eating one is not hungry.

3 你隻眼見乜野呢 Nei₂ chek₀ ngaan₂ kin° mat⁴ ye₂ ni¹?

3 What is the matter with your eyes?

4 我兩晚都唔瞓得，今晚見好眼瞓 Ngoh₂ leung₂ maan₂ to¹ m₁ fan⁰ tak₄ kam¹ maan₂ kin⁵ ho² ngaan₂ fan³.

4 I have not slept well for two nights and my eyes are very sleepy this evening.

5 你眼有冇見痛 Nei₂ ngaan₂ yau₂ mo₂ kin³ t'ung⁷.

5 Do your eyes feel sore.

6 唔係，我兩隻耳見痛係真嘅 M₁ hai₃, Ngoh₂ leung₂ chek₀ i₂ kin⁵ t'ung⁸ hai₃ chan¹ ke.³

6 No, but really my ears are painful.

7 呢幾日，有牙痛冇 Ni¹ kei² yat₄ yau₂ ngai t'ung⁵ mo₂?

7 These few days have you had tooth ache?

8 你啲手指好番未 Nei₂ ti¹ shau² chi² ho² faan¹ mei₃.

8 Is your finger well yet?

9 我自前日見痛，今日好番 Ngoh₂ tsz₃ ts'in₁ yat₄ kin° t'ung⁸, kam¹ yat₄ ho² faan¹.

9 For the last two days I have had pain, but to-day I am well.

10 我自己話，老人係咁，手腳或耳，時時有一樣痛. Ngoh₂ tsz₃ kei² wa₃, lo₂ yan₁ hai₃ kom², shau² keuk₀ wak₄ i₂ shi₁ shi₁ yau₂ yat⁴ yeung₃ t'ung⁷.

10 I myself say, old people are so, either their hands or feet or ears are always sore.

英粵通語 Cantonese for everyone ——香港大學粵語教材（一九三一）

69

The Twenty-ninth Exercise---(Conversation.)

1 Good morning, Why have I not seen you the last few days?
Tso² shan₁, tim² kaai² ni¹ kei² yat₄ mo₂ kin³ nei₂?
早晨點解呢幾日冇見你

2 These few days I have not been very well.
Ngoh₂ ni¹ kei² yat₄ m₁ bai₅ kei² ho².
我呢幾日唔係幾'好．

3 What is the matter? Have you eaten too much?
Yau₂ mat⁴ sz₃ ni¹? Hai₃ shik₄ tak⁴ toh¹ kwoh⁸ t'au₁ m₁ hai₃?
有乜事呢,係食得多過頭唔係．

4 It is partly that. I ate too much and had stomach ache.
Yau₂ shiu² shiu² hai₃, ngoh₂ shik₄ tak⁴ toh¹ kwoh³ t'au₁,
tsau₃ t'o₂ t'ung³. 有少少係,我食得多過頭,就肚痛．

5 Why did you not listen (attend) to what we said about eating?
Tim² kaai² koh² yat₄ kong² shik₄ nei₂ m₁ t'eng¹ ni¹?
點解个日講食你唔聽呢

6 That evening I was asked to a feast. The things were most excellent
and I ate a good deal.
Koh² maan₂ yau₂ yan₁ kiu³ ngoh₂ hui⁵ yam², ti¹ ye₂
m₁ chi¹ kei² ho² shik₄, ngoh₂ shik₄ ho² toh¹.
个晚有人叫我去飲,啲野唔知幾好食,我食好多．

7 Why did you eat so much?
Tim² kaai² nei₂ shik₄ kom⁹ toh¹ ni¹? 點解你食咁多呢．

8 Need that be told? Every one, seeing good food, always eats and eats too much
Chung₃ shai² kong² *ke⁵, yan₁ yan₁ kin³ ye₂ ho² shik₄,
shi₁ shi₁ to¹ hai₃ yat⁴ shik₄, shik₄ toh¹ kwoh³ t'au₁.
重使講嘅,人人見野好食,時時都係一食,食多過頭．

9 Why are you so foolish?
Tim² kaai² nei₂ kom⁵ mo₂ 'kin³ shik⁴ ni¹?
點解你咁冇見識呢．

10 I do not know. Really it may be said that I am foolish.
Ngoh₂ to¹ m₁ chi¹ to⁵, chan¹ hai₃ wa₃ tak⁴ mo₂ kin⁵
shik⁴ lok₀. 我都唔知到,真係話得冇見識略．

11 If you know you are foolish, what will you do?
Nei₂ chi¹ nei₂ mo₂ kin¹ shik⁴, nei₂ iu⁸ tim² *yeung₂?
你知你冇見識你要點樣．

12 Being foolish, one must give one's mind to study, that is it.
Mo₂ kin³ shik⁴ tsau₃ yung₂ sam¹ hok₄, ye₂ hai₃ la¹.
冇見識'就用心學野係喇

THE THIRTIETH LESSON

第 三 十 課—Tai₃ saam¹ shap₄ foh³

1	苦	Foo'—*Bitter, pain, grief.*
2	辛	San¹—*Pungent, acrid.*
3	力	Lik₄—*Strength.*
4	勤	K'an₁—*Industrious.*
5	勢	Shai'—*Power, conditions.*
6	懶	Laan₂—*Lazy.*
7	惰	Toh₈—*Reluctant, slow.*
8	蠢	Ch'un²—*Foolish.*
9	精	Tsing¹—*Smart, energetic, energy.*
10	神	Shan₁—*Spirit, energy.*

1 佢見口苦,都見口乾. K'ui₂ kin' hau² foo², to¹ kin⁵ hau² kon¹.

His mouth is bitter, and also dry.

2 佢兒得好辛苦. K'ui₂ kin' tak⁴ ho² san¹ foo².

He has much pain.

3 佢係唔係冇力呢. K'ui₂ hai₃ m₁ hai₃ mo₂ lik₄ ni¹?

Has he no strength?

4 唔係,佢好勤力. M₁ hai₃, k'ui₂ ho² k'an₁ lik₄.

No, he is very industrious, (hard working).

5 舊時有个人好大勢力. Kau₃ shi₁ yau₂ koh³ yan₁ ho² taai₃ shai³ lik₄.

Formerly there was a man, who had great power.

6 佢係懶做工唔係. K'ui₂ hai₃ laan₂ tso₃ kung¹ m₁ hai₃?

Is he lazy (at work)?

7 係,佢好懶惰嘅. Hai₃, k'ui₂ ho² laan₂ toh₈ ke³.

Yes, he is very lazy.

8 點解佢咁蠢呢. Tim² kaai² k'ui₂ kom° ch'un² ni¹?

Why is he so foolish?

9 佢重話好精. K'ui₂ chung₃ wa₃ ho² tsing¹?

Yet he says (he is) very smart.

10 冇精神唔做得工. Mo₂ tsing¹ shan₁ m₁ tso₃ tak⁴ kung¹.

(If) one has no energy one cannot work.

The Thirtieth Exercise—(Conversation.)

1 To-day I am really feeling unwell.

Kam¹ yat₄ chan¹ hai₃ san¹ foo². 今日真係辛苦

2 Why are you so·ill (painful)?

Tim² kaai² kom⁵ san¹ foo² ni¹ ? 點解咁辛苦呢

3 Yesterday I told you the reason.

Tsok₄ yat₄ ngoh₂ wa₇ choh² nei₂ chi¹ tim² kaai² lok₀

昨 日 我 話 嘅 你 知 點 解 略

4 What, you ate too much and you are not even better now.   Is that so ?

Mat⁴ a³, shik₄ ye₂ toh¹ kwoh⁵ t'au₁, chung₈ mei₃ ho² faan¹, hai₃ m₁ hai₈ ni¹ ?

乜呀,食野多過頭,重未好番,係唔係呢.

5 Yes, certainly, up to the present I am not yet well.

Hai₇, *ting₃ lok₀, to¹ mei₃ ho² faan¹

係 定 略, 都 未 好 番

6 So hard to get well; What did you eat that day ?

Kom³ naan₁ ho² ke³, nei₂ koh² yat₄ shik₄ ti¹ mat⁴ ye₂ ni¹ ?   咁 難 好 嘅, 你 个 日 食 啲 乜 野 呢

7 I have told you I ate a great many things.

To¹ wa, shik₄ ho² toh¹ ye₂ lok₀.   都話食好多野略

8 Can you tell me how many things you ate ?

Kong² tak⁴ ngoh₂ t'eng¹ nei₂ shik₄ kei² toh¹ ye₂ m₁ ni¹ ?

講 得 我 聽 你 食 幾 多 野 唔 呢

9 I can not tell you how many things I ate.

Shik₄ choh² kong² m₁ ch'ut⁴ kom³ toh¹.

食 嘅 講 唔 出 咁 多

10 I do not think you are sick.   It is but laziness.

Ngoh₂ t'ai² nei₂ m₁ hai₇ yau₂ sz₇, pat⁴ kwoh⁵ laan₂ toh₃

我 睇 你 唔 係 有 事, 不 過 懶 惰

11 Am I lazy? I am very diligent. I really (have no energy).

Ngoh₂ laan₂ toh₃ a¹? Ngoh₂ ho² k'an₁ lik₄ ke³, mo₂ tsing¹ shan₁ tsau₇ hai₈ chan¹.

我懶惰吖!我好勤力嘅,有精神就係真

12 Diligence is good, do not be lazy. (practice laziness).

K'an₁ lik₄ hai₃ ho², m₁ ho² hok₄ laan₀ toh₂.

勤 力 係 好, 唔 好 學 懶 惰

THE THIRTY FIRST LESSON

第 三 十 一 課—Tai₃ saam¹ shap₄ yat⁴ foh³.

1	醫	I¹—*Cure, doctor.*	6	險	Him²—*Dangerous, risk.*
2	病	Peng₅—*Sick, disease*	7	傷	Sheung¹—*Wound, injure.*
3	藥	Yeuk₄—*Medicine.*	8	咪	Mai₂—*Do not.*
4	死	Sz₂² (see,² say²)—*Die, dead.*	9	聲	Sheng¹—*Sound, voice.*
5	危	Ngai₁—*Dangerous.*	10	氣	Hei²—*Breath, anger*

1 佢係醫生 K'ui₂ hai₃ i¹ shang¹.

1 He is a doctor.

2 病人要請醫生 Peng₅ yan₁ iu⁵ ts'ing² i¹ shang¹.

2 Sick people must send for a doctor to see them.

3 醫生時時俾好苦嘅藥水過病人飲 I¹ shang¹ shi₄ shi₄ pei² ho² foo² ke⁶ yeuk₄ shui² kwoh⁵ peng₃ yan₁ yam².

3 The doctor always gives very bitter medicine to the patients to drink.

4 冇人想死嘅 Mo₂ yan₁ seung² sz² ke³.

4 No one wants to die.

5 佢嘅病係好危 K'ui₂ ke³ peng₃ hai₃ ho² ngai₁.

5 His condition is critical.

6 有啲病係好危險嘅 Yau₂ ti¹ peng₃ hai₃ ho² ngai₁ him² ke³.

6 Some diseases are very dangerous.

7 我見一个人喺街俾貨車車傷 Ngoh₂ kin³ yat⁴ koh⁵ yan₁ hai² kaai¹ pei² foh³ ch'e¹ ch'e¹ sheung¹.

7 I saw a man in the street injured by a motor lorry.

8 你咪俾病人傷心至好 Nei₂ mai₂ pei² peng₃ yan₁ sheung¹ sam¹ chi³ ho².

8 Do not allow sick people to be worried (that is best).

9 佢唔講得好大聲 K'ui₂ m₁ kong² tak⁴ ho² taai₃ sheng¹.

9 He cannot speak very loud.

10 你睇佢重有氣冇 Nei₂ t'ai² k'ui₂ chung₃ yau₂ hei³ mo₂.

10 You see whether he still has any breath.

The Thirty-first Exercise—(Conversation.)

1 Good morning, are you well (again) to-day?

Tso² shan₁, kam³ yat₄ ho² faan¹ mei, ni¹?

早晨, 今日好番未呢

2 I am not yet well. I still have to see the doctor, (need the doctor to see me).

Mei₃ ho² faan¹, chung₈ iu³ i¹ shang¹ t'ai² chi² tak⁴.

未好番, 重要醫生睇至得

3 What! are you still taking medicine?

Mat⁴, nei₂ chung₈ shik₄ yeuk₄? 乜你重食藥

4 Yes, being sick, I must take medicine.

Hai₁ a¹, yau₂ peng₃ tsau₃ iu³ shik₄ yeuk₄.

係吓, 有病就要食藥

5 (If you) did not take (medicine) what would happen?

M₁ shik₄ tsau₃ tim² ni¹? 唔食就點呢

6 (If I) did not take medicine (I) would die.

M₁ shik₄ yeuk₄ tsau₁ sz² lok₀. 唔食藥就死咯

7 You cannot die so soon. Do you say you are in a critical condition? (Is that so)?

M₁ sz² tak⁴ kom³ faai³, nei₂ wa₃ ho² ngai₁, hai₃ m₁ hai₁ ni¹? 唔死得咁快, 你話好危, 係唔係呢.

8 It may not be very serious, If I were ill I could not walk, but I am still not out of danger.

M₁ hai₁ yat⁴ teng₃ ke³, ngai₁, tsau₃ m₁ haang₁ tak⁴ lok₀, taan₈ hai₃ to¹ yau₂ him².

唔係一定嘅. 危就唔行得咯. 但係都有險.

9 What danger is there? You are not injured.

Ngai₁ him² mat⁴ ye₂? Nei₂ mo₂ shau₁ sheung¹ a¹?

危險乜野, 你冇受傷吓.

10 Well, injured, I am not injured, do not talk so much.

Sheung¹, mo₂ mat⁴ sheung¹, mai₂ kong² kom³ toh¹.

傷冇乜傷, 咪講咁多

11 You are really long winded.

Nei₂ chan¹ hai₃ ch'eung₁ hei³. 你真係長氣.

12 I am not long-winded (tedious).

Ngoh₂ m₁ hai₈ ch'eung₁ hei³ a¹. 我唔係長氣吓.

THE THIRTY-SECOND LESSON

第 三 十 二 課—Tai₃ saam¹ shap₄ i₃ foh³

1	巾	Kan¹—*Towel, handkerchief.*	6	除	Ch'ui₃ or ch'ue₁—*Take off or away.*
2	毛	Mo₁—*Hair, hairy.*	7	衣	I¹—*Clothes.*
3	氊	Chin¹—*Blanket, felt.*	8	服	Fuk₄—*Serve, submit, I¹ fuk₄, clothes.*
4	帽	*Mo₃—*Hat.*	9	櫃	*Kwai₃—*Coffer, chest.*
5	擦	Ch'aat₀—*Brush, rub*	10	床	Ch'ong₁—*Bed*

1 拧一條手巾仔嚟俾我.
Ning¹ yat⁴ t'iu₁ shau² kan¹ tsai² lai₁ pei² ngoh₂.

1 Bring me a handkerchief.

2 我要毛巾洗面. Ngoh₂ iu³ mo₁ kan¹ sai² min₃.

2 I want a towel to wash my face.

3 今晚好熱我唔要氊.
Kam¹ *maan₂ ho² it₄ ngoh₂ m₁ iu³ chin¹.

3 It is very hot to-night. I do not want a blanket.

4 你擦我件氊帽去做乜野
Nei₂ ning¹ ngoh₂ kin₃ chin¹ *mo₃ hui³ tso³ mat⁴ ye₂ ?

4 Why did you take my felt hat away.

5 我拧你件氊帽去擦.
Ngoh₂ ning¹ nei₂ kin₃ chin¹ *mo₃ hui³ ch'aat₀.

5 I took your felt hat to be brushed.

6 熱過頭,我一定要除衫.
It₄ *kwoh³ t'au₁ ngoh₂ yat⁴ teng₃ iu³ ch'ue₁ shaam¹.

6 It is too hot, I must take off my coat.

7 落雨个時 有雨衣唔使濕身.
Lok₄ ue₂ koh² shi₁, yau₂ ue₂ i¹ m₁ shai¹ shap⁴ shan¹.

7 When it rains if one has a raincoat one will not get wet.

8 你擠我的衣服喺邊處.
Nei² chai¹ ngoh₂ ti¹ i¹ fuk₄ hai² pin¹ shue³.

8 Where did you put my clothes ?

9 我擠你的衣服喺櫃.
Ngoh₂ chai¹ nei₂ ti¹ i¹ fuk₄ hai² kwai₃.

9 I put your clothes in the wardrobe.

10 眞係眼瞓咯,我想卽時去床瞓?
Chan¹ hai₃ ngaan₂ fan³ lok₀, ngoh₂ seung² tsik⁴ shi₁ hui³ ch'ong₁ fan³.

10 I am really sleepy, I want to go to bed at once.

The Thirty-second Exercise—(Conversation.)

1 What did you buy when you went out yesterday ?

'Tsok₄ yat₄ nei₂ hui⁵ kaai¹ maai₂ mat⁴ ye₂ ?

昨日你去街買乜野.

2 I went to buy some towels.

Ngoh₂ hui³ maai₂ ti¹ mo₁ kan¹.　我去買的毛巾.

3 Did you buy anything else ?

Chung₋ yau₂ maai₂ mat⁴ ye₂ mo₂ ?　重有買乜野冇.

4 Yes, I bought a felt hat.

Yau₂, ngoh₂ maai₂ choh² yat⁴ kin₃ chin¹ *mo₃.

有，我買咧一件氈帽.

5 Felt hats are not very good, one must always brush them, and always take off one's hat.

Chin¹ *mo₃ m₁ hai₅ kei² ho², iu³ shi₁ shi₁ ch'aat₀, shi₁ shi₁ ch'ui₁ *mo₃. 氈帽唔係幾好, 要時時擦, 時時除帽

6 Where do you put your clothes ?

Nei₂ ti¹ i¹ fuk₄ chai¹ pin¹ shue³ ?

你的衣服擠邊處.

7 I put them in the wardrobe.

Ngoh₂ chai¹ hai² kwai₃.　我擠喺櫃

8 In which wardrobe did you put them ?

Chai¹ hai² pin¹ koh³ kwai₃.　擠喺邊个櫃

9 In the large wardrobe near the bed.

Hai² ch'ong₁ pin¹ koh² koh³ taai₅ kwai₃.

喺床邊个个大櫃

10 Why can I not open the door of the wardrobe ?

Tim² kaai² kwai₃ moon₁ m₁ hoi¹ tak⁴ ke³ ?

點解櫃門唔開得嘅

11 I could open it just now.

Ngoh₂ sin¹ t'au₁ to¹ hoi¹ tak⁴.　我先頭都開得.

12 Really I cannot open it.

Ngoh₂ chan¹ hai₃ m₁ hoi¹ tak⁴.　我真係唔開得.

THE THIRTY THIRD LESSON

第 三 十 三 課—Tai₃ saam¹ shap₄ saam¹ foh³

1	晒	Shaai⁵—*Dry in the sun.*
2	搣	K'aai₂—*Carry take, bring.*
3	遮	Che¹—*Shade, shelter umbrella.*
4	抹	Maat₀ or moot₀—*Wipe, dust.*
5	鏡	Keng⁵—*Mirror, Looking-glass*
6	洋	Yeung₁—*Ocean, foreign.*
7	皮	*P'ei₁—*Skin, leather, fur.*
8	鞋	Haai₁—*Shoes.*
9	熨	T'ong³—*To iron.*
10	斗	Tau²—*A measure, Vessel.*

1 點解你个面晒得咁黑呢? Tim² kaai' nei₂ koh³ min₃ shaai' tak⁴ kom³ hak⁴ ni¹?

1 Why is your face so dark?

2 佢搣的紙嚟寫字 K'ui₂ k'aai₂ ti¹ chi² lai₁ se² tsz...

2 He used the paper to write on.

3 你要用帽至得，唔係要用遮 Nei₂ iu yung₃ mo₃ chi tak', m₁ hai₃ iu⁵ yung₃ che.¹

3 You must wear a hat If not, you must use an umbrella (instead of a hat.)

4 我去街買布抹檯 Ngoh₂ hui³ kaai' maai₂ po³ maat₀ *t'oi₁.

4 I went out to buy some cloth for dusting the table.

5 你唔睇吓个鏡 Nei₂ m₁ t'ai² ha₂ koh³ keng⁵?

5 Why do you not look in a glass.

6 有人話洋貨好 Yau₂ yan₁ wa₃ yeung₁ foh³ ho².

6 Some people say foreign goods are good.

7 今日你嘅皮黑嘔咯 Kam¹ yat₁ nei₂ ke' p'ei₁ hak⁴ choh² lok₀.

7 To-day your skin is quite dark.

8 一定冇皮鞋咁黑 Yat⁴ teng₃ mo₂ p'ei₁ haai₁ kom³ hak⁴.

8 It is certainly not so black as boots.

9 呢件衫要熨至得，你用乜嚟熨呢 Ni¹ kin₃ shaam₁ iu⁵ t'ong³ chi³ tak¹, nei₂ yung₃ mat¹ ye₂ t'ong³ ni¹?

9 This coat must be ironed. What will you use to iron it?

10 用電熨斗係快的 Yung₃ tin₁ t'ong¹ tau⁴ hai₃ faai¹ ti¹.

10 It is quicker to use an electric iron.

The Thirty-third Exercise—(Conversation)

1 Why is your face so red to day?

Kam¹ yat₄ nei₂ koh³ min₃ tso₃ mat⁴ kom³ hung₁ ni¹?

今 日 你 個 面 做 乜 咁 紅 呢.

2 Yes, I have just drunk a great deal.

Hai₃, ngoh₂ tsau₃ chi³ yam² ho² toh¹.

係，我 就 至 飲 好 多.

3 How much did you drink?

Yam² tak⁴ kei² toh¹ ni¹? 飲 得 幾 多 呢.

4 I drank a great deal and as I drank I kept wiping my face with a handkerchief.

Yam²ho² toh¹, yat⁴ lo₃ yam², yat⁴ lo₃ yung₃ shau² kan¹ maat₀ min₃. 飲 好 多，一 路 飲，一 路 用 手 巾 抹 面.

5 Then it would certainly be red. I think you must have been in the sun.

Kom² tsau₃ yat⁴ teng₃ hung₁ lok₀, ngoh₂ t'ai² yau₂ it₄ *t'au₁ shaai³ to¹ m₁ teng₃.

咁 就 一 定 紅 咯，我 睇 有 熱 頭 晒 都 唔 定.

6 I must look into a mirror.

Ngoh₂ iu³ yung₃ keng⁹ t'ai² ha₂. 我 要 用 鏡 睇 吓.

7 Do you say it is as red as foreign cloth?

Nei₂ wa₃ hai₃ m₁ hai₃ yeung₁ po³ kom³ hung₁ ni¹?

你 話 係 唔 係 洋 布 咁 紅 呢.

8 It is pretty red. The skin is red.

To¹ hai₃ kei² hung₁, ti¹ p'ei₁ hung₁ a³.

都 係 幾 紅 ，啲 皮 紅 呀.

9 One must not expose oneself to the sun, and make one's skin so black (dark).

To¹ hai₃ m₁ ho² shaai³ kom³ hak⁴ ke³.

都 係 唔 好 晒 咁 黑 嘅.

10 Yes, without a hat one may be scorched to a black colour.

Hai₃ mo₂ *mo₃ stau₃ shaai³ tak⁴ ho² hak⁴.

係 ，冇 帽 就·晒 得 好 黑.

THE THIRTY-FOURTH LESSON

第 三 十 四 課—Tai₃ saam¹ shap₄ sz³ foh³

1 光 Kwong¹—*Light, bright.*	**6** 糟 Tso¹—*Residue, dregs*
2 鮮 Sin¹—*Fresh.*	**7** 換 Oon₃—*Change.*
3 試 Shi¹—*Try, test, examine.*	**8** 動 Tung₃—*Move, movement.*
4 靚 Leng³—*Pretty, beautiful.*	**9** 衞 Wai₃—*Protect,* (Wai₃ shaang¹) *sanitary.*
5 污 Oo¹—*Dirty.*	**10** 合 Hop₄—*Right, exact, agree.*

1 電燈光過油燈. Tin₃ tang¹ kwong¹ kwoh⁸ yau₁ tang¹.

1 Electric lamps are brighter than oil lamps.

2 佢嘅衫熨得好光鮮. K'ui₂ ke³ shaam¹ t'ong³ tak⁴ ho² kwong¹ sin¹.

2 His coat is ironed very well (bright and fresh).

3 你試吓用電熨斗. Nei₂ shi⁰ ha₂ yung₃ tin₃ t'ong³ tau².

3 You try an electric iron.

4 真係熨得好靚. Chan¹ hai₃ t'ong³ tak⁴ ho² leng³.

4 Really it irons very well.

5 你嘅面有啲污點. Nei₂ ke³ min₃ yau₁ ti¹ oo¹ tim².

5 There are some dirty spots on your face.

6 係,真係好污糟. Hai₃, chan¹ hai₃ ho² oo¹ tso¹.

6 Yes, really it is very dirty

7 做乜你今朝唔換檯布呢 T'so₃ mat⁴ nei₂ kam¹ chiu¹ m₁ oon₃ *t'oi₁ po⁸ ni¹?

7 Why did you not change the table cloth this morning?

8 我起身晏有時候運動. Ngoh₂ hei² shan¹ aan' mo₂ shi₁ hau wan₁ tung₋.

8 I got up late and did not have time for exercise. '

9 地方冇衞生人就生病. Tei₃ fong¹ mo₂ wai₃ shaang¹ yan₁ tsau₃ shaang¹ peng₃

9 If the place is not sanitary people will get sick.

10 係吖, 唔合衞生就生病. Hai₃ a¹, m₁ hop₄ wai₃ shang¹ tsau₃ shaang¹ peng₃.

10 Yes, if the place is not sanitary, people will become sick

The Thirty-fourth Exercise—(Conversation.)

1 It is dawn. Get up.

T'in[1] kwong[1] lok[0], hei[2] shan[1] a[1]. 天光咯,起身吖

2 Well, to-day we must buy some thing fresh to eat.

Ho[2] a[1], kam[1] yat[4] iu[3] maai[2] ti[1] san[1] sin[1] ye[2] shik[4].

好吖, 今日要買啲新鮮野食

3 Try to get a little veal for food.

Shı ha[2] maai[2] ti[1] ngau[1] tsai[2] yuk[4] shik[4] ha[2].

試吓買啲牛仔肉食吓

4 All is useless (false), you must sweep the place clean.

Mat[4] tc[1] hai[3] ka[2], so[3] tseng[3] ti[1] tei[3] fong[1] chi[3] tak[4].

乜都係假,掃淨啲地方至得

5 All right, How nice your coat is ?

Tak[4] lok[0], mat[4] nei[2] kin[3] shaam[1] kom[3] leng[3] *ke[3] ?

得 咯, 乜你件衫咁靚嘅

6 Yes, it is pretty good (bright and fresh)· It is newly bought

To[1] hai[3] kei[3] kwong[3] sin[1], hai[3] san[1] maai[2] ke[3].

都 係 幾 光 鮮, 係 新 買 嘅

7 It seems to me that you have ironed it.

Ngoh[2] t'ai[2] nei[2] pei[2] t'ong[3] tau[2] t'ong[3] kwoh[3].

我 睇 你 俾 熨 斗 熨 過

8 Yes, how keen your eyes are !

Mat[4] nei[2] kom[3] ho[2] ngaan[2] ke[3] ! 乜你咁好眼嘅

9 That place is very dirty.

Koh[1] ti[3] tei[3] fong[1] ho[2] oo[1] tso[1]. 个啲地方好污糟

10 Yes. it is not healthy, you must sweep it.

Hai[3], ho[2] m[1] hop[4] wai[3] shaang[1], iu[3] so[3] kwoh[3] chi[3] tak[4]

係好唔合衞生,要掃過至得

11 Yes, tell some one to come quickly and clean it.

Hai[3] lok[0], kiu[3] yan[1] faai[3] ti[1] lai[1] so[3] la[1].

係 咯, 叫 人 快 啲 嚟 掃 喇

12 Ah muk, go quickly and sweep the floor.

Ah muk[4], nei[2] faai[3] ti[1] hui[3] so[3] tei[3].

亞 木, 你 快 啲 去 掃 地

香港・澳門雙城成長經典

80

THE THIRTY-FIFTH LESSON

第 三 十 五 課—Tai₃ saam¹ shap₁ ng₂ foh²

1	嚟	Ooi₂—Can, able, will	6	臭	Ch'au²—Foul, stinking.
2	剃	T'ai³—Shave, cut, dress hair.	7	梘	Kaan²—Soap
3	鬚	So¹—Beard.	8	香	Heung¹—Fragrant.
4	剪	Tsin²—Cut with scissors, shear.	9	頂	Teng²—Top.
5	髮	Faat₀—Hair.	10	籃	*Laam₁—Basket.

1 佢嚟㗎唔嚟？ K'ui₂ ooi₂ lai₁ m₁ ooi₂.

1 Will he come or not ?

2 你嚟剃頭唔嚟. Nei₂ ooi₂ t'ai³ t'au₁ m₁ ooi₂.

2 Can you dress hair ?

3 我唔嚟剃頭,我嚟剃鬚. Ngoh₂ m₁ ooi₂ t'ai³ t'au₁ ngoh₂ ooi₂ t'ai³ so¹.

3 I cannot dress hair but I can shave my beard.

4 佢剪乜野呢. K'ui₂ tsin² mat⁴ ye₂ ni¹ ?

4 What is he cutting (with scissors) ?

5 佢剪髮. Kiu₂ tsin² faat₀.

5 He is cutting hair.

6 你洗頭係落臭水洗唔係 Nei₂ sai² t'au² hai₃ lok₄ ch'au³ shui² sai² m₁ hai₃.

6 Do you wash your head with disinfectant ?

7 唔係,我洗頭用梘洗. M₁ hai₃, ngoh₂ sai² t'au² yung₃ kaan² sai³.

7 No, I use soap to wash my head.

8 上等香梘好香. Sheung₂ tang² heung¹ kaan² ho² heung¹.

8 The best scented soap is very fragrant.

9 好多人掉臭水去山頂賣. Ho² toh¹ yan₃ ning¹ ch'au³ shui² hui³ shaan¹ teng⁴ maai₃.

9 Many people take disinfectant to the Peak to sell.

10 佢用籃掉去賣嘅. K'ui₃ yung₃ *laam₁ ning¹ hui³ maai₃ ke³.

10 He carries it with basket (to sell).

81

The Thirty-fifth Exercise—(Conversation.)

1   What news is there to-day ?
     Kam¹ yat₄ yau₂ mat⁴ san¹ *man₁ ?
     今 日 有 乜 新 聞

2   There is, China is prepared for war.
     Yau₂ a¹, chung¹ kwok₀ seung² ta².   有吖,中國想打

3   Why should China fight ?
     Tim² kaai² iu³ ta² ni¹ ?   點 解 要 打 呢?

4   They say, they must fight.
     Kui₂ tei₃ wa₃, m₁ ta² m₁ tak⁴.
     佢 地 話, 唔 打 唔 得

5   Why do they all want to fight ?
     Tim² kaai³ k'ui₂ taai₃ chung³ iu² ta² ni¹?
     點 解 佢 大 衆 要 打 呢?

6   Will they certainly do so later ?
     K'ui₂ tei₃ hau₃ loi₁ yat⁴ ting₈ iu³ kom° *yeung₃ tso₈ me¹?
     佢 哋 後 來 一 定 要 咁 樣 做 (咩)

7   Some people say there will be no fighting soon.
     Yau₂ yan₁ wa₃ mo₂ kei² *noi₃ tsau₈ mo₂ tak⁴ ta².
     有 人 話 冇 幾 耐 就 冇 得 打

8   I also hope that they will not fight.
     Ngoh₂ to¹ seung² k'ui₂ tei₃ m₁ ho² ta².
     我 都 想 佢 哋 唔 好 打

9   The corpses on the battlefield smell very bad.
     Ta² sz² ti¹ yan₁ ho² ch'au³ ke⁸.
     打 死 的 人 好 臭 嘅

10   Yes, but after disinfecting them there is no offensive smell.
     Hai₋ taan₃ hai₃ yung₃ yeuk₄ shui² tsau₃ m₁ ooi₂ ch'au².
     係, 但 係 用 藥 水 就 唔 嚹 臭

THE THIRTY SIXTH LESSON

第 三 十 六 課—Tai₉ saam¹ shap₄ luk₄ foh³

1	羊	Yeung₁—*Sheep, goat.*	6	蛋	*Taan₃—*an egg.*
2	奶	Naai₂—*Milk.*	7	狗	Kau²—*Dog.*
3	猪	Chue¹—*Pig.*	8	貓	Maau¹—*Cat.*
4	骨	Kwat⁴—*Bone.*	9	鼠	Shue²—*Rat.*
5	雞	Kai¹—*Fowl.*	10	味	Mei₃—*Flavour, taste.*

1. 你食羊肉唔食 Nei₂ shik₄ yeung₁ yuk₄ m₁ shik₄?
   Do you eat mutton?

2. 我食羊肉都飲牛奶 Ngoh₂ shik₄ yeung₁ yuk₄ to¹ yam² ngau₁ naai₂.
   I eat mutton and also drink cow's milk.

3. 猪肉好食定牛肉好食呢 Chue¹ yuk₄ ho² shik₄ teng₃ ngau₁ yuk₄ ho² shik₄ ni¹?
   Is pork better to eat or beef?

4. 牛肉好食,猪肉冇骨都係好食 Ngau₁ yuk₄ ho² shik₄, chue¹ yuk₃ mo₂ kwat⁴ to¹ hai₃ ho² shik₄.
   Beef is good to eat, pork without bones is also good to eat.

5. 雞肉係好食過牛肉 Kai¹ yuk₄ hai₃ ho² shik₄ kwoh³ ngau₁ yuk₄.
   Chicken is better to eat than beef.

6. 朝朝我食三隻雞蛋 Chiu¹ chiu¹ ngoh₂ shik₄ saam¹ chek₀ kai¹ *taan₃.
   Every morning I eat three eggs.

7. 我屋企有一隻狗睇門口 Ngoh₂ uk⁴ k'ei² yau₂ yat¹ chek₀ kau² t'ai² moon₁ hau².
   In my house I have a dog to watch the door.

8. 前日佢買咗一隻三色貓 T'sin₁ yat₄ k'ui₂ maai₂ choh² yat⁴ chek₀ saam¹ shik⁴ maau¹.
   The day before yesterday he bought a three coloured cat.

9. 貓嗬食老鼠 Maau¹ ooi₂ shik₄ lo₂ shue².
   Cats are able to eat rats.

10. 雞肉真係好味 Kai¹ yuk₄ chan¹ hai₃ ho² mei₃.
    The flesh of fowls really tastes good.

The Thirty-sixth Exercise—(Conversation.)

1 Yesterday I bought three goats.

Tsok₄ vat₄ ngoh₂ maai₂ saam¹ chek₀ *yeung₁.

昨 日 我 買 三 隻 羊

2 Why did you buy them?

Maai₂ lai₁ tso₃ mat⁴ ye₂ ni¹? 買 嚟 做 乜 野 呢

3 Having bought them I shall have goat's milk to drink.

Maai₂ choh² tak⁴ yeung₁ naai₁ lai₁ yam².

買 咗 得 羊 奶 嚟 飲

4 Is goat's milk good to drink?

Yeung₁ naai₂ ho² yam² m₁ ni¹? 羊 奶 好 飲 唔 呢

5 Pretty good. Some people say it is better than cow's milk

Kei² ho² yam², yau₂ yan₁ wa₃ ho² yam² kwoh³ ngau₁ naai₂. 幾 好 飲, 有 人 話 好 飲 過 牛 奶

6 Why does every one drink cow's milk, and not goat's milk?

Tim² kaai² yan₁ yan₁ yam² ngau₁ naai₂ m₁ yam² yeung₁ naai₂ ni¹? 點 解 人 人 飲 牛 奶 唔 飲 羊 奶 呢

7 I do not know why, but some people drink goat's milk.

Ngoh₁ m₁ chi¹ tim² kaai². taan₃ hai₃ to¹ yau₂ yan₁ yam² yeung₁ naai₂. 我 唔 知 點 解, 但 係 都 有 人 飲 羊 奶

8 (The customs of) all countries are different, Some people eat pork, some people eat dog's flesh.

Yat⁴ *kwok₀ kwok₀ m₁ t'ung₁ ke³, yau₂ yan₁ shik₄ chue¹ yuk₄, yau₂ yan₁ shik₄ kau² yuk₄.

一 國 國 唔 同 嘅, 有 人 食 猪 肉, 有 人 食 狗 肉

9 I have heard some people say that there are some men who eat rats.

Ngoh₂ t'eng¹ yan₁ kong², yau₂ yan₁ shik₄ lo₂ shue² to¹ yau₂. 我 聽 人 講, 有 人 食 老 鼠 都 有

10 I do not know whether they are good to eat or not. Eggs are better to eat than many things however.

M₁ chi¹ ho² shik₄ m₁ ho², taan₃ hai₃ kai¹ *taan₃ ho² shik₄ kwoh³ ho² toh¹ yeung₄.

唔 知 好 食 唔 好, 但 係 雞 蛋 好 食 過 好 多 樣

84

THE THIRTY SEVENTH LESSON

第 三 十 七 課—Tai₃ saam¹ shap₁ ts'at¹ foh˙

1	餐	Ts'aan¹—*A Meal.*	6	刀	To¹—*Knife.*
2	湯	T'ong¹—*Soup.*	7	义	Ch'a¹—*Fork.*
3	羹	Kang¹—*Spoon.*	8	酒	Tsau²—*Wine.*
4	碟	Tip₄—*Plate.*	9	壺	Oo₁—*Pot.*
5	碗	Oon²—*Bowl.*	10	杯	Pui¹—*Cup.*

1 你幾點鐘食餐呢 Nei₂ kei² tim² chung¹ shik₄ ts'aan¹ ni¹?

1 When do you take your meal?

2 你食餐有飲湯冇呢 Nei₂ shik₄ ts'aan¹ yau₂ yam² t'ong¹ mo₂ ni¹?

2 When you eat your meal do you take soup?

3 有,我用羹嚟飲湯 Yau₂, ngoh₂ yung₄ kang¹ lai₁ yam² t'ong¹.

3 Yes, I use a spoon to take soup.

4 西人用碟食餐係唔係呢 Sai¹ yan₁ yung₃ tip₄ shik₄ ts'aan¹ hai₃ m₁ hai₃ ni¹?

4 Do Europeans use plates to serve their meals?

5 係,唐人用碗多,都有用碟 Hai₃, t'ong₁ yan₁ yung₃ oon² toh¹, to¹ yau₂ yung₃ tip₄.

5 Yes, Chinese mostly use bowls to eat their food, some also use plates.

6 西人用刀食肉係唔係呢 Sai¹ yan₁ yung₃ to¹ shik₄ yuk₄ hai₃ m₁ hai₃ ni¹?

6 Do Europeans use knives to cut meat (at meals?)

7 係,西人用刀叉 Hai₃, sai¹ yan₁ yung₃ to¹ ch'a².

7 Yes, Europeans use knives and forks to eat with.

8 你食飯有飲酒冇 Nei₂ shik₄ faan₃ yau₂ yam² tsau² mo₂?

8 When you eat rice do you drink wine?

9 茶壺大過酒壺 Ch'a₁ oc₁ taai₃ kwoh³ tsau² oc₁.

9 Teapots are larger than wine-pots.

10 西人飲酒用大水杯,唐人用細酒杯 Sai¹ yan₁ yam² tsau² yung₃ taai₃ shui² pui¹, t'ong₁ yan₁ yung₃ sai³ tsau² pui¹.

10 Europeans take wine with glasses, Chinese drink wine with small wine cups.

The Thirty-seventh Exercise—(Conversation.)

1 To-day it would be well to talk of eating.

Kam¹ yat₄ kong² ha₂ shik₄ to¹ ho² a¹

今 日 講 吓 食 都 好 吖

2 Very well, do Europeans and Chinese take their food in different ways?

Ho² a¹, Sai¹ yan₁ shik₄ ye₂ m₁ t'ung₁ t'ong₁ yan₁ hai₃ m₁ hai₃ ni¹ ?　好吖,西人食野唔同唐人係唔係呢

3 Yes, they are different in many ways.

Hai₃, ho² toh¹ ye₂ to¹ m₁ t'ung₁.

係, 好 多 野 都 唔 同

4 Europeans serve soup in plates.

Sai¹ yan₁ yam² t'ong¹ yung₃ *tip₄.

西 人 飲 湯 用 碟

5 Some people cannot distinguish whether the food they eat is good or bad.

Yau₂ ti¹ yan₁ shik₄ ye₂ to¹ m₁ chi¹ ti¹ ye₂ ho² m₁ ho².

有 啲 人 食 野 都 唔 知 啲 野 好 唔 好

6 He requires to drink a lot of water every day.

K'ui₂ yat₄ yat₄ iu³ yam² ho² toh¹ shui².

佢 日 日 要 飲 好 多 水

7 Does he take soup.

Yau₂ yam² t'ong¹ mo₂ ni¹ ?　有 飲 湯 冇 呢

8 Yes, he takes soup with a large spoon, he eats his meal with knives and forks.

Yau₂, k'ui₂ yam² t'ong¹ yung₃ taai³ kang¹, shik₄ ts'aan¹ yung₃ to¹ ch'a¹.　有,佢飲湯用大羹,食餐用刀叉

9 He drinks water and soup. Does he drink wine ?

Yam² shui² yam² t'ong¹, yau₂ yam² tsau₂ mo₂ ni¹ ?

飲 水 飲 湯, 有 飲 酒 冇 呢

10 Yes, he always drinks several large glasses of wine.

Yau₂, k'ui₂ shi₁ shi₁ yam² kei² taai₃ pui¹ tsau².

有, 佢 時 時 飲 幾 大 杯 酒

香港・澳門雙城成長經典

THE THIRTY-EIGHTH LESSON

第 · 三 十 八 課—Tai_3 $saam^1$ $shap_4$ $paat_0$ foh^8

1	切	$Ts'it_0$—*Cut, mince.*	6	麥 Mak_4—*Wheat.*
2	餅	$Peng^2$—*Cake.*	7	菓 $Kwoh^2$—*Fruit.*
3	粉	Fan^2—*Powder, flour,*	8	糖 $T'ong_1$—*Sugar.*
4	麵	Min_3—*Wheaten.*	9	鹽 Im_1—*Salt.*
5	飽	$Paau^1$—*Cake, bread.* $Paau^2$—*Repletion.*	10	鹹 $Haam_1$—*Briny, salt taste.*

1 小心切至好,唔係噲切親手. Siu^2 sam^1 $ts'it_0$ chi^3 ho^2, m_1 hai_3 ooi_2 $ts'it_0$ $ts'an^1$ $shau^2$.

1 One must be careful in cutting, or else one may cut one's hand.

2 邊個搦咁多餅嚟. Pin^1 koh^3 $ning^1$ kom^3 toh^1 $peng^2$ lai_1 ?

2 Who brought so many cakes here?

3 呢啲係乜野粉. Ni^1 ti^1 hai_3 mat^4 ye_2 fan^2 ?

3 What kind of powder is this ?

4 个啲係麵粉. Koh^2 ti^1 hai_3 min_3 fan^2.

4 That is wheaten flour.

5 麵粉要嚟整麵飽. Min_3 fan^2 iu^3 lai_1 $ching^2$ min_3 $paau^1$.

5 Flour is used to make bread.

6 今朝我食咗一大碗牛奶麥粉. Kam^1 $chiu^1$ $ngoh_2$ $shik_4$ $choh^2$ yat^4 $taai_3$ oon' $ngau_1$ $naai_2$ mak_4 fan^2.

6 This morning I ate a large bowl of oatmeal and milk.

7 人人都話生菓係好食. Yan_1 yan_1 to^1 wa_3 $shaang^1$ $kwoh^2$ hai_3 ho^2 $shik_4$.

7 Everyone says fresh fruit is good to eat.

8 食糖菓唔使落糖. $Shik_4$ $t'ong_1$ $kwoh^2$ m_1 $shai^2$ lok_4 $t'ong_1$.

8 One need not add sugar to jam when eating it.

9 个啲湯冇味嘅,我要落鹽. Koh_2 ti^1 $tong^1$ mo_2 mei_3 ke^3, $ngoh_2$ iu^3 lok_4 im_1.

9 That soup is tasteless, I want to add salt to it.

10 唔好落咁多鹽唔係噲鹹過頭. M_1 ho^2 lok_4 kom^3 toh^1 im_1 m_1 hai_3 ooi_2 $haam_1$ $kwoh_3$ $t'au_1$.

10 Do not put in so much salt, or it will be too briny.

The Thirty-eighth Exercise—(Conversation.)

1 Are there any other differences between Europeans and Chinese in ways of taking food?

Sai¹ yan₁ t'ung₁ t'ong₁ yan₁ shik₄ ye₂ chung₃ yau₂ mat⁴ fan₁ pit₄ ni¹?

西人同唐人食野重有乜分別呢

2 Yes, a great many. I have heard some people say they differ in many ways.

Yau₂, ho² toh¹, ngoh₂ t'eng¹ yan₁ kong² koh² ti¹ ye₂ tsau₅ ho² toh¹ m₁ t'ung₁.

有好多,我聽人講个哟野就好多唔同

3 What are the differences?

Tim² *yeung₃ m₁ t'ung₁ ni¹? 點樣唔同呢

4 We eat rice whilst they eat bread cutting it into slices.

Ngoh₂ tei₃ shik₄ faan₃, k'ui₂ tei₃ shik₄ min₃ paau¹, ts'it₀ hoi¹ yat⁴ *faai³ faai³ shik₄.

我哋食飯,佢哋食麵飽,切開一塊塊食

5 What else?

Chung₃ yau₂ ni¹? 重 有 呢

6 It is more than I can tell. We use bowls. They mostly use plates.

M₁ kong² tak⁴ kom³ toh¹, ngoh₂ tei₃ yung₃ oon², k'ui₂ tei₃ yung₃* tip₄ toh¹.

唔講得咁多,我哋用碗,佢哋用碟多

7 They eat porridge. Is that good or not?

K'ui₂ tei₃ shik₄ mak₄ fan² ho² m₁ ho² ni¹?

佢 哋 食 麥 粉 好 唔 好 呢

8 It is good. Many Chinese also eat oatmeal (porridge).

Ho², t'ong₁ yan₁ ho² toh¹ to³ shik₄ mak₄ fan².

好, 唐 人 好 多 都 食 麥 粉

9 Do the Chinese eat porridge with sugar or salt?

T'ong₁ yan₁ shik₄ mak₄ fan² lok₄ t'ong₁ teng₅ lok₄ im₁ ni¹?

唐人食麥粉落糖定落鹽呢

10 It depends upon what they like, sometimes they add sugar and sometimes salt.

Me₂ yat⁴ teng₅ ke⁴, yau₂ shi₁ lok₄ t'ong₁ yau₂ shi₁ lok₄ im₁. 冇一定嘅有時落糖有時落鹽

THE THIRTY NINTH LESSON

第 三 十 九 課--T̆ai₃ saam¹ shap, kaau² foh'

1	機	Kei¹—*Machine, loom.*
2	器	Hei³—*Vessel, utensil, apparatus.*
3	飛	Fei¹—*To fly.*
4	搭	Taap₀—*To take passage.*
5	站	Chaam₃—*A station.*
6	向	Heung³—*Towards, direction, formerly.*
7	停	T'ing₁—*Stop.*
8	壞	Waai₃—*Destroy, damage.*
9	尾	Mei₂—*Tail, end.*
10	擺	Paai²—*Spread out, more.*

1 呢啲係乜野機呢 Ni¹ ti¹ hai₃ mat⁴ ye₂ kei¹ ni¹?
2 个啲係機器 Koh² ti¹ hai₃ kei¹ hei⁵.
3 係飛機唔係 Hai₃ fei¹ kei¹ m₁ hai;.
4 唔係,你想搭飛機唔想呢 M₁ hai₃, nei₂ seung² taap, fei¹ kei¹ m₁ seung² ni¹?
5 想嘅,但唔知有站冇呢 Seung² ke³, taan₃ m₁ chi¹ yau₂ chaam₃ mo₂ ni¹?
6 飛機向站落要細心 飛近站就要慢車 Fei¹ kei¹ heung₃ chaam₃ lok₄, iu³ sai³ sam¹, fei¹ kan₃ chaam₃ tsau³ iu³ maan₃ ch'e¹.
7 到站停車,但有個站唔停車 T̆o³ chaam₃ t'ing₁ ch'e¹, taan₃ yau₂ koh° chaam₃ m₁ t'ing₁ ch'e¹.
8 車壞必要停車嚟整好 Ch'e¹ waai₃ pit⁴ iu³ t'ing₁ ch'e¹ lai₁ ching² ho².
9 車尾有紅燈 Ch'e¹ mei₂ yau₂ hung₁ tang¹.
10 車尾兩頭擺,就好危險嘞 Che¹ mei₂ leung₂ t'au¹ paai², tsau₃ ho² ngai₁ him² lok₀.

1 What kind of machine is this?
2 That is an engine.
3 Is it a flying machine?
4 No, do you wish to ride in an aeroplane?
5 I wish to, but do not know whether there are any stations.
6 Aeroplanes approaching a station must descend carefully, when near the aerodrome they must go slowly.
7 A station being reached, the train stops. It, however, does not stop at all stations
8 If the engine is out of order it must be stopped and repaired.
9 At the rear of the train there is a red light.
10 A violent swing at the rear of a train is very dangerous,

89

The Thirty-ninth Exercise—(Conversation.)

1 I have not seen you for a long time. Where have you been?
M₁ kin³ kom³ noi₃, nei₂ hui³ pin¹ shue⁵ ?
唔 見 咁 耐, 你 去 邊 處

2 I have been to Shanghai.
Ngoh₂ hui⁵ sheung₅ hoi². 我 去 上 海

3 How do you go to Shanghai, can you go there by train?
Hui¹ sheung₅ hoi² tim² hui³ ni¹? Yau₂ foh² ch'e¹ hui³ mo₂ ni¹? 去 上 海 點 去 呢 ? 有 火 車 去 冇 呢 ?

4 No, one must go by steamer, sometimes aeroplanes are also available.
Mo₂ iu⁵ ts'o¹ ₂foh²shuen₁. nei₅chung¹to¹yau₂fei¹kei¹.
冇, 要 坐 火 船, 內 中 都 有 飛 機.

5 Are there stations for aeroplanes?
Fei¹ kei¹ yau₂ mo₂ chaam₃ ni¹? 飛 機 有 冇 站 呢

6 Sometimes there are, if you fly a long distance.
Yau₂ *shi₁ yau₂, fei¹ hui³ uen₂ ke⁷ tei₂fong¹tsau₃yau₂.
有 時 有, 飛 去 遠 嘅 地 方 就 有

7 Is Shanghai far from here?
Hui³ sheung₃ hoi² uen₂ m₁ uen₂ ni¹?
去 上 海 遠 唔 遠 呢

8 Three days by water.
Saam¹ yat₄ shui² lo₃. 三 日 水 路

9 The engines of aeroplanes often go wrong.
Fei¹ kei¹ kei¹ hei³ shi₁ shi₁ waai₃.
飛 機 機 器 時 時 壞

10 That is certainly so, but very seldom.
Koh² ti¹ yat⁴ ting₃ yau₂, taan₅ hai₃ ho² shiu².
个 啲 一 定 有, 但 係 好 少

11 I often hear people say they are out of order.
Ngoh₂ shi₁ shi₁ t'eng¹ van₁ kong² wa₃ yau₂ waai₃.
我 時 時 聽 人 講 話 有 壞

12 Yes, sometimes when the steering apparatus is not properly controlled it causes damage.
Hai, ke³, yau₂ shi₁ paai² mei₂ m₁ ho² tsau₁ yau₂.
係 嘅, 有 時 擺 尾 唔 好 就 有

THE FORTIETH LESSON

第 四 十 課—Tai₃ sz⁵ shap₄ foh³

1	緊 Kan²—*Important, tight*	6	穩 Wan²—*Safe*
2	急 Kap⁴—*Urgent, haste*	7	覺 Kok₀—*Realize, feel*
3	極 Kik₄—*Extreme*	8	不 Pat⁴—*Not*
4	太 T'aai³—*Too*	9	能 Nang₁—*Able*
5	驚 Keng¹—*Fear, afraid*	10	曬 Saai⁵—*All* Saai¹—*Waste*

---

1 呢件事好緊要. Ni¹ kin₃ sz₃ ho² kan² iu⁵.

1 This affair is very important.

2 係好急嘅唔係吖. Hai₃ ho² kap⁴ ke³ m₁ hai₃ a¹ ?

2 Is it very urgent ?

3 係極急定略. Hai, kik₄ kap⁴ *ting₃ lok₀.

3 Yes, certainly, extremely urgent.

4 你講得太緊要. Nei₁ kong² tak⁴ t'aai³ kan² iu⁵.

4 You overstate the matter.

5 你重唔驚,驚乜野呢. Nei₂ chung₃ m₁ keng¹ l keng¹ mat⁴ ye₂ ni¹ ?

5 Are you still not afraid? Afraid of what ?

6 呢處好唔穩陣. Ni¹ shue³ ho² m₁ wan² chan₃.

6 It is very unsafe here.

7 我唔覺得有乜野. Ngoh₂ m₁ kok₀ tak⁴ yar₂ mat⁴ ye₂.

7 I do not notice anything.

8 我先頭見佢,但不覺就唔見咗佢咯. Ngoh₂ sin¹ t'au₁ kin³ k'ui₂, taan₃ pat⁴ kok₀ tsau₃ m₁ kin⁵ choh² k'ui₂ lok₀ !

8 I saw him a short time ago, but, without noticing it. I have lost sight of him.

9 真係唔見佢,但係佢不能去得幾遠嘅. Chan¹ hai₃ m₁ kin³ k'ui₂, taan₃ hai₃ k'ui₂ pat⁴ nang₁ hui³ tak⁴ kei₂ uen₂ ke³.

9 Is he really lost? He cannot however have gone very far.

10 佢嘅野都唔見曬. K'ui₂ ke³ ye₂ to¹ m₁ kin³ saai³.

10 All his belongings have also disappeared.

The Fortieth Exercise—(Conversation.)

1 What is your hurry to-day ?

Kam¹ yat₁ yau₂ mat⁴ kan² kap⁴ sz₃ ni¹ ?

今 日 有 乜 緊 急 事 呢

2 I must look for an aeroplane to go to Shanghai.

Ngoh₂ iu³ wan² fei¹ kei¹ ts'oh₂ hui³ sheung, hoi².

我 要 搵 飛 機 坐 去 上 海

3 It is not very good. To ride in an aeroplane is too dangerous

M₁ ho², fei¹ kei¹ t'aai⁷ him².

唔 好, 飛 機 太 險

4 It is not very dangerous, I cannot wait as I must try to find one.

M₁ hai₃ kei² him², ngoh₂ pat⁴ nang₁ tang², tsau₃ iu³ hui³ wan². 唔係幾險,我不能等,就要去搵

5 Why are you in such a hurry ? It is extremely dangerous.

Mat⁴ kom³ kap⁴ ni¹? hai₃ kik₄ ngai₁ him² a¹.

乜 咁 急 呢, 係 極 危 險 吖

6 I am not afraid. The matter being very urgent I must go at once.

M₁ p'a³, ti¹ sz₃ kik₄ kan², tsau₃ iu³ hui⁵.

唔 怕, 的 事 極 緊, 就 要 去

7 Do you wish to risk your life ? Do you not want to live ? or do you want to die ?

Nei₂ m¹ seung⁷ shang¹ me¹? 你 唔 想 生 咩

8 Are you really so afraid ?

Nei₂ chan¹ hai₂ kom³ p'a³? 你 真 係 咁 怕

9 Are you really not afraid ?

Nei₂ chan¹ hai₃ m₁ p'a³? 你 真 係 唔 怕

10 Yes, I am not afraid at all.

Hai₃, ngoh₂ tsau₃ m₁ p'a³ lok₆.

係, 我 就 唔 怕 咯

THE FORTY FIRST LESSON

第 四 十 一 課—Tai₃ sz³ shap₁ yat⁴ foh³.

1	應	Ying¹—*Ought, promise.*	6 德	Tak⁴—*Virtue.*
2	當	Tong¹—*Ought.* Tong³—*Regard as, pawn.*	7 各	Kok₀—*Each, every, all.*
3	該	Koi¹—*Ought, that.*	8 家	Ka¹—*Family.*
4	守	Shau²—*Retain, preserve.*	9 規	K'wai¹—*Custom, rule, compasses.*
5	道	To,—*Principles, doctrine.*	10 矩	Kui²—*Custom, rule, (squares).*

1 人人應要勤力學野
Yan₁ yan₁ ying¹ iu³ k'an₁ lik₄ hok₄ ye₂

1 Every one ought to study hard.

2 學野應當用心 Hok₄ ye₂ ying¹ tong¹ yung³ sam¹.

2 In learning, one ought to exercise one's mind.

3 唔該你解俾我知點樣用心
M₁ koi¹ nei₂ kaai² pei² ngoh₂ chi¹ tim² 'yeung₃ yung₃ sam¹⁹

3 Please explain to me how one can exercise one's mind.

4 你守住章程做就得咯
Nei₂ shau² chue₃ cheung¹ ch'ing₁ tso₃, tsau₃ tak⁴ lok₀

4 If you keep the regulations, it will do.

5 先生教學生要有人道
Sin¹ shaang¹ kaau³ hok₄ shaang¹ iu³ yau₂ van₁ to₃

5 The teacher teaches the students philanthropy.

6 守道德就有好德行
Shau² to₃, tak⁴ tsau₃ yau₂ ho² tak⁴ hang₃.

6 If one keeps right principles one's conduct is good.

7 唔明白道理嘅人各樣都唔知
M₁ ming₁ paak₄ to₃ lei₂ ke³ yan₂ kok₀ veung₃ to¹ m₁ chi¹.

7 People who do not understand right principles know nothing.

8 佢講家事就好聽
K'ui₂ kong² ka¹ sz₃ tsau₃ ho² t'eng¹.

8 He speaks about family affairs it is good to hear him.

9 當你細个个陣時你嘅親要你守家規 Tong¹ nei₂ sai³ koh³ koh³ chan₃ shi₁, nei₂ mo₂ t'san¹ iu³ nei₂ shau² ka¹ k'wai¹.

9 When you were young your mother made you adhere to family rules.

10 去處處都應該守規矩
Hui³ shue³ shue³ to¹ ying¹ koi¹ shau² k'wai¹ kui².

10 Wherever you go you ought to obey the rules of the place.

The Forty-first Exercise—(Conversation.)

1 You do not look very well, do not work so hard.
Ngoh$_2$ t'ai^2 nei$_2$ t'aai^3 san^1 foo^2, m$_1$ ho^2 kom^3 lok$_4$ lik$_4$.
我睇你太辛苦，唔好咁落力

2 No, I only do what I ought to do.
M$_1$ hai$_3$, Ngoh$_2$ pat^4 kwoh^3 tso$_3$ tong^1 tso$_3$ ke^3 kung^1.
唔係，我不過做當做嘅工

3 I think you ought not to do so much.
Ngoh$_2$ wa$_3$ m$_1$ ying^1 koi^1 tso$_3$ kom^3 toh^1.
我話唔應該做咁多

4 I say I must do so much. I cannot leave it undone.
Ngoh$_2$ wa$_3$ yat^4 ting$_3$ iu^3 tso$_3$ kom^3 toh^1, m$_1$ tso$_3$ m$_1$ tak^4
我話一定要做咁多．唔做唔得

5 Why cannot you leave it undone? (what is the necesity?)
Yau$_2$ mat^4 m$_1$ tso$_3$ m$_1$ tak^4 ni^1? 有乜唔做唔得呢

6 Virtue is man's greatest necessity.
Yan$_1$ chi^3 kan^2 iu^3 ke^3 sz$_3$ hai$_3$ kong$_2$ to$_3$ lei$_2$.
人至緊要嘅事：係講道理

7 I say you speak unreasonably.
Ngoh$_2$ wa$_3$ nei$_2$ kong^2 tak^4 ho^2 mo$_2$ to$_3$ lei$_2$.
我話你講得好冇道理

8 You may say what you like, I think I must do it.
Nei$_2$ yau$_2$ nei$_2$ kong^2, ngoh$_2$ kok$_0$ tak^4 hai$_3$ iu^3 tso$_3$.
你有你講，我覺得係要做

9 If your health is injured you can do nothing.
Nei$_2$ sheung^1 choh^2 ti^1 tsing^1 shan$_1$, kom^2 mat^4 to^1 m$_1$ tso$_3$ tak^4 a^3. 你傷啫啲精神，咁乜都唔做得呀

10 I have heard people say "man is never killed by work."
Ngoh$_2$ t'eng^1 yan$_1$ kong^2 tso$_3$ kung^1 mo$_2$ sheung^1 sz^2 yan$_1$ ke^3 我聽人講，做工冇傷死人嘅

11 It depends upon what work he does, out-door work is not injurious to health. Office work is more injurious.
T'ai^2 mat^4 ye$_2$ kung^1 a^3, hai^2 ngoi$_3$ pin$_3$ tso$_3$ m$_1$ p'a^3, se^2 tsz$_3$ chung$_3$ sheung^1 tak^4 yan$_1$ toh^1.
睇乜野工呀，喺外便做唔怕，寫字重傷得人多．

THE FORTY-SECOND LESSON

第 四 十 二 課—Tai₃ sz³ shap₄ i₃ foh³

1	姓	Sing³—*Surname.*	6	辭 T'sz₁ — *Resign, dismiss, deny.*
2	名	Meng₁ (meng³)—*Name.*	7	可 Hoh²—*Able, can, may.*
3	齊	Ts'ai₁—*All, even, equal*	8	所 Shoh²—*That which,* ("Shoh²" *is a Chinese pronoun*)
4	答	Taap₀—*Reply*	9	以 I₂—*With*
5	公	Kung¹—*Public, male.*	10	司 Sz¹—*Control, superintend, an officer*

1 先生高姓呀？ Sin¹ shaang¹, ko¹ sing³ a³?

1 Sir, what is your surname?
(Note in speaking to workmen one often says) Nei₂ sing³ mat⁴, kiu³ mat⁴ *meng₂* ni¹? What is your surname and name?

2 小姓文，名百新 Siu² sing³ man₁, meng₁ paak₀ san¹.

2 My surname is Man₁ and my name Paak₁ San¹.

3 有人問你一齊嘅事你點樣呢. Yau₂ yan₁ man₃ nei₂ yat⁴ ts'ai₁ ke³ sz₃ nei₂ tim² yeung₃ ni¹?

3 If one asks you all about affairs, what will you do?

4 我要答番佢. Ngoh₂ iu³ taap₀ faan¹ k'ui₂.

4 I must answer him.

5 佢喺寫字樓有乜公事 K'ui₂ hai₃ se² tsz.lau₁ yau₂ mat⁴ kung¹ sz₃.

5 In what capacity is he in the office.

6 舊時佢喺寫字樓做打字，但係後尾俾人開辭 K'au₃ shi₁ k'ui₂ hai₃ se² tsz₃ lau₁ tso₃ ta² tsz₃. taan₃ hai₃ hau₂ mei₂ pei² yan₁ hoi¹ ts'z₁

6 Formerly he was in the office in the capacity of typist. But afterwards he was dismissed.

7 你可能帶佢去文先生處搵工唔呢. Nei₂ hoh² nang₁ taai³ k'ui, hui³ man₁ sin¹ shaang¹ shue² wan² kun₀¹ m₁ ni¹.

7 Can you take him to Mr. Man's place and find some work for him to do?

8 你所講都怕係好嘅, Nei₂ shoh² kong² to¹ p'a³ hai₃ ho² ke².

8 What you say is also good, I think.

9 後日你可以帶佢去文先生處搵工. Hau₁ yat₄ nei₂ hoh² i₂ taai³ k'ui₂ hui³ man₁ sin¹ shaang¹ shue³ wan² kung¹.

9 The day after to-morrow you may take him to Mr. Man's place to find some work (for him to do.)

10 佢近來冇工做所以我想搵一間公司俾工佢做. K'ui₂ kan₃ loi₁ mo₂ kung¹ tso₃ shoh² i₂ ngoh₂ seung² wan² yat⁴ kaan¹ kung¹ sz¹ pei² kung¹ k'ui₂ tso₃.

10 Of late he is out of work and I therefore wish to find some company which will give him work.

The Forty-second Exercise—(Conversation.)

1 How many people are there in your office ?

Nei₂ kaan¹ se² tsz₃ lau₁ yau₂ kei² toh¹ yan₁ ni¹ ?

你 間 寫 字 樓 有 幾 多 人 呢 ?

2 Altogether there are sixty people.

Kung₀ maai₁ yau₂ luk₄ shap₄ yan₁ a¹.

共 埋 有 六 十 人 吖

3 I heard you had dismissed ten.

Ngoh₂ man₁ tak⁴ nei₂ t'sz₁ choh² yau₂ shap₄ koh³ yan₁

我 聞 得 你 辭 唨 有 十 个 人

4 Yes, I sent off ten lately.

Hai₃. Kan₃ yat₄ ngoh₂ t'sz₁ choh² shap₄ koh³ yan₁.

係, 近 日 我 辭 唨 十 个 人

5 Why did you send so many at once ?

Tim² kaai² nei₂ yat⁴ *ts'ai₁ t'sz₁ kom³ toh¹ yan₁ ni¹ ?

點 解 你 一 齊 辭 咁 多 人 呢

6 Everything is too dear, therefore I cannot employ so many.

Yeung₃ yeung₃ ye₂ t'aai³ kwai³, shoh² i₂ m₁ ts'ing² tak⁴ kom³ toh¹ yan₁. 樣 樣 野 太 貴, 所 以 唔 請 得 咁 多 人

7 Two or three of them are my relations, could you take them back?

Yau₂ leung₂ saan ¹koh³ hai₃ ngoh₂ ts'an¹ van₁ nei₂ hoh²i₂ ts'ing² faan¹ k'ui₂ m₁ ni¹? 有 兩 三 个 係 我 親 人 你 可 以 請 番 佢 唔 呢

8 Exchange is so uncertain that business is very difficult.

Ngan₁ shui² kom³ mɔ₂ ting₃, maai₂ maai₃ kik₄ naan₁.

銀 水 咁 冇 定, 買 賣 極 難

9 You might do what you can for me and take them on again ?

Nei₂ hoh² i₂ t'ai² ngoh₂ min₃ sheung₃ ts'ing² faan¹ k'ui₂ tak⁴ m₁ tak⁴ ni¹ ? 你 可 以 睇 我 面 上, 請 番 佢 得 唔 得 呢

10 If I take them on again, I must send away others.

Ngoh₂ hai₃ ts'ing² faan¹ k'ui₂ iu₃ ts'z₁ tai₃ i₃ ti¹ yan₁.

我 係 請 番 佢, 要 辭 第 二 的 人

11 The others may not be so badly off.

Tai₃ i₃ ti¹ yan₁ p'a³ mo₂ kom³ naan₁ ke₃.

第 二 的 人 怕 冇 咁 難 嘅

12 I must be just in my affairs.

Ngoh₂ tso₃ sz₅ to¹ iu₃ kung¹ to₃ chi³ tak⁴ a¹.

我 做 事 都 要 公 道 至 得 吖

THE FORTY THIRD LESSON

第 四 十 三 課—Tai₃ sz³ shap₄ saam¹ foh⁸.

1	料	Liu—*Surmise, material, calculate.*		
2	通	Tung¹—*Penetrate, whole, to reach to, open, clear.*		
3	嘅	Pe₃—*Or.*		
4	啱	Ngaam¹—*Exact, right.*		
5	主	Chue²—*Owner, master.*		
6	意	I³—*Idea, meaning.*		
7	思	Sz³—*Idea, thought.* Sz¹—*Think, consider.*		
8	疑	I₁—*Doubt.*		
9	材	Ts'oi₁—*Materials, qualities.*		
10	必	Pit⁴—*Must, certainly.*		

1　我料唔到个个人係咁好
Ngoh₂ liu₃ m₁ to⁸ koh² koh⁴ yan₃ hai₃ kom³ ho².

1 I did not think that man was so good.

2　你真係唔通 Nei₂ chan¹ hai₃ m₁ t'ung¹.

2 You are certainly dull.

3　唔知你錯嘅我錯呢? M₁ chi¹ nei₂ ts'oh⁸ pe₃ ngoh₂ ts'oh³ ni¹?

3 I do not know whether you are wrong or I?

4　我係啱定喇, 我識佢好耐
Ngoh₂ hai₃ ngaam¹ teng₃ la¹ ngoh₂ shik⁴ k'ui₂ ho² nois₃.

4 Certainly I am right. I have known him for a long time.

5　我識佢有幾耐, 係佢做主唔呢
Ngoh₂ shik⁴ k'ui₂ mo₂ kei⁴ nois, hai₃ k'ui₂ tso₃ chue² m₁ ni¹?

5 I know him but recently. Is he the leader?

6　係, 係佢做主意 Hai₃, hai₃ k'ui₂ tso₃ chue² i⁸.

6 Yes, he decides every thing.

7　佢有乜野意思呢 K'ui₂ yau₂ mat⁴ ye₂ i³ sz³ ni¹?

7 What is his idea?

8　我思疑佢唔好心 Ngoh₂ sz¹ i₁ k'ui₂ m₁ ho² sam¹.

8 I think he is an evil hearted man.

9　呢啲材料唔好 Ni¹ ti¹ ts'oi₁ *liu₃ m₁ ho².

9 These materials are bad.

10　必定係咁嘅咯 Pit⁴ ting₃ hai₃ kom² ke³ lok₆.

10 It must be so.

Other words for "or" are waak₄—see list after lesson 12—and tengs but very frequently a slight "a" sound is given between two sentences to denote "or".

The Forty-third Exercise—(Conversation.)

1 Good morning, Sir, I have not seen you for a long time.
Sin¹ shaang¹, tso² shan₁, ho² noi₃ m₁ kin³.
先 生, 早 晨, 好 耐 唔 見

2 I do not remember whether I have seen you before.
M₁ chi¹ kau₃ shi₁ yau₂ kin³ kwoh³ mo₂.
唔 知 舊 時 有 見 過 冇

3 I think you do not believe me.
Ngoh₂ koo² sin¹ shaang¹ p'a³ yau₂ sz¹ i₁ a¹.
我 估 先 生 怕 有 思 疑 吖

4 What you think is right. When did I see you?
Nei₂ koo² tak⁴ ngaam¹, ngoh₂ kei² shi₁ kin³ kwoh³ nei₂
ni¹? 你 估 得 啱, 我 幾 時 見 過 你 呢.

5 Did I not see you in that new company the year before last?
Ts'in₁ *nin₁ hai² koh² kaan¹ san¹ kung¹ sz¹ m₁ hai₃
kin² kwoh³. 前年喺个間新公司唔係見過?

6 Sorry!
Chan¹ m₁ ho² i³ sz³. 真 唔 好 意 思

7 Do not say that, it was only that you did not notice it.
M₁ ho² kom² kong², sin¹ shaang¹ pat⁴ kwoh³ m₁ tsoi₃
i³ che¹. 唔 好 咁 講, 先 生 不 過 唔 在 意 啫

8 Yes, at that time you were young and now your appearance has changed.
Hai₃ a¹, nei₂ koh² shi₁ hai₃ hau₃ shaang¹ in₃ kam¹
yau₂ koi² pin³. 係吖,你个時係後生現今有改變

9 Quite so. Many people say so. Some friends cannot recognize me.
Mo₂ ts'oh³, ho² toh¹ yan₁ hai₃ kom² wa₃, yau₂ p'ang₁
yau₂ m₁ shik⁴ ngoh₂.
冇錯, 好多人係咁話, 有朋友唔識我

10 Certainly, it is so.
Pit⁴ ting₃ hai₃ yau₂ kom³ *yeung₃. 必 定 係 有 咁 樣

THE FORTY-FOURTH LESSON

第 四 十 四 課—Tai₃ sz³ shap₄ sz³ foh⁵

1	恭	Kung¹—*Respect, congratulate.*	6	送	Sung³—*Attend, escort.*
2	喜	Hei²—*Glad.*	7	喪	Song¹—*Funeral.* Song¹—*To lose.*
3	歡	Foon¹—*Happy.*	8	費	Fai³—*Expense.*
4	結	Kit₀—*Combine.*	9	謝	Tse₅—*Thank.*
5	婚	Fan¹—*Marriage.*	10	笑	Siu³—*Laugh.*

1 恭字嘅意思係有禮.
Kung¹ tsz₃ ke³ i⁵ sz³ hai₃ yau₂ lai₂

1 By respect is meant good manners.

2 新年頭多人話恭喜你
San¹ nin₁ t'au₁ toh¹ yan₁ wa₃ kung¹ hei² nei₂.

2 In the new year "Happy New Year" is a common greeting.

3 有錢佬時時好歡喜.
Yau₂ *ts'in₁ lo² shi₁ shi₁ ho² foon¹ hei².

3 The rich are always happy.

4 佢結識一个西人朋友.
K'ui₂ kit₀ shik⁴ yat⁴ koh³ sai¹ yan₁ p'ang₁ yau₂.

4 He has made acquaintance with an European.

5 結婚係一件極歡喜嘅事 Kit₀
fan¹ hai₃ yat⁴ kin₃ kik₄ foon¹ hei² ke³ sz₃.

5 Marriage is a very happy event

6 佢係去送船唔係. K'ui₂
hai₃ hui³ sung³ shuen₁ m₁ hai₃?

6 Has he gone to a ship to see a friend off?

7 唔係 佢去送喪. M₁ hai₃,
k'ui₂ hui³ sung⁸ song¹.

7 No, he has gone to attend a funeral.

8 送船有送喪咁貴事.
Sung³ shuen₁ mo₂ sung⁸ song¹ kom³ fai³ sz₃.

8 Seeing a friend off is not so troublesome as attending a funeral.

9 有人送禮俾你 你要話多謝
Yau₂ yan₁ sung⁵ lai₂ pei² nei₂, nei₂ iu³ wa₃ toh¹ tse₃.

9 When your friend makes you a present you must say "many thinks."

10 你笑佢做乜野. Nei₂
siu⁸ k'ui₂ tso₃ mat⁴ ye₂.

10 Why do you laugh at him?

The Forty-fourth Exercise—(Conversation.)

1 Where are you working, Sir ?

Sin¹ shaang¹, kung¹ hei² hai² pin¹ shue³ ?

先 生, 恭 喜 喺 邊 處

2 I am working in that large house.

Ngoh₂ hai² koh² kaan¹ taai₃ uk⁴ ch'ut⁴ yap₁ toh¹.

我 喺 个 間 大 屋 出 入 多

3 I have heard a wedding will take place there.

Man₁ tak⁴ koh² shue³ yau₂ yan₁ kit₀ fan¹.

聞 得 个 處 有 人 結 婚

4 It is true, I am going to send them a present.

Hai₁ chan¹ ke³, ngoh₂ tsau₃ hui³ sung³ lai₂ pei₁ k'ui₂.

係 真 嘅, 我 就 去 送 禮 俾 佢

5 What a happy event it is ! I am just doing the opposite.

Chan¹ yau₂ kom³ hei² foon¹ ke³ sz₃ ! Ngoh₂ tsau₃ seung¹ faan² lok₀.

真 有 咁 喜 歡 嘅 事! 我 就 相 反 略

6, What is that ? Are you going to attend a funeral ?

Tim² a¹, sung³ song¹ hai₃ ma³ ?

點 吖, 送 喪 係 嗎

7 Yes, what a troublesome thing it is !

Hai₃ lok₀, ni¹ ti¹ hai₃ ho² fai³ sz₃ !

係 略, 呢 啲 係 好 費 事

8 Yes, but they are very grateful to you.

Hai₃ ke³, taan₃ k'ui₂ ho² toh¹ tse₃ nei₂.

係 嘅, 但 佢 好 多 謝 你

9 Yes, both families are grateful.

Hai₅, leung₂ ka¹ to¹ yau₂ tse₅. 係, 兩 家 都 有 謝

10 Human affairs are really funny (you congratulate your friend on his marriage whilst I attend a funeral).

Chan¹ hai₃ ngob₂ tei₃ yan₁ sz₃ hai₃ ho² siu³

真 係 我 哋 人 事 係 好 笑

THE FORTY FIFTH LESSON

第 四 十 五 課—Tai₃ sz³ shap₄ ng₂ foh³.

1	奇	K'ei₁—*Strange.*
2	別	Pit₄—*Distinguish, other.*
3	特	Tak₄—*Special, purposely.*
4	種	Chung²—*Seed, kind, class* Chung³—*To plant*
5	改	Koi²—*Change, repent*
6	裝	Chong¹—*Style, to pack*
7	箱	Seung¹—*Box, case*
8	輕	Hing¹—*light*
9	子	Tsz² or chi²—*Son, small*
10	毫	Ho₁—*A ten cent, piece*

1 呢嘅事咁奇 你可以解得出唔
呢 Ni¹ ti¹ sz₃ kom³ k'ei₁ nei₂
hoh²i₂ kaai² tak⁴ ch'ut⁴ m₁ ni¹?

1 Can you explain matters which are so strange ?

2 唔可以 個的事極難分別嘅.
M₁ hoh² i₂, koh² ti¹ sz₃ kik₄
naan₁ fan¹ pit, ke³.

2 I cannot, those things are very difficult to distinguish.

3 个啲野咁難分別係好特別唔呢
Koh² ti¹ ye, kom³ naan₁ fan¹
pit₄, hai₃ ho² tak₄ pit₄ m₁ ni¹?

3 Being so difficult to distinguish, are those very peculiar things?

4 唔係好特別, 不過種數太多.
M₁ hai₃ ho² tak₄ pit₄, pat⁴
kwoh³ chung² sho³ t'aai³ toh¹.

4 Not very peculiar, but there are many kinds of them.

5 船期有改冇呢. Shuen₁
k'ei₁ yau₂ koi² mo₂ ni¹?

5 Is the date of sailing changed?

6 船期冇改你要裝定貨.
Shuen₁ k'ei₁ mo₂ koi², nei₂
iu³ chong¹ ting₃ foh³.

6 The date of sailing is not changed, you must get the goods ready.

7 係用箱裝貨唔係. Hai₃
yung₃ seung¹ chong¹ foh³ m₁ hai₃?

7 Will the goods be packed in cases ?

8 舊時箱裝, 就用輕箱.
Kau₃ shi₁ seung¹ chong¹
tsau₃ yung₃ hing¹ seung¹

8 Formerly we packed them in cases, so pack them in light cases.

9 隻船乜野日子開身呢.
Chek₃ shuen₁ mat⁴ ye₂ yat₄
tsz² hoi¹ shan¹ ni¹ ?

9 When will the ship sail?

10 我買六毫子野. Ngoh₂
maai₂ luk₁ ho₁ tsz² ye₂.

10 I bought sixty cents worth of things.

The Forty-fifth Exercise—(Conversation.)

1 Good morning, Sir. Where are you going so early?

Tso² shan₁, siu¹ shaang¹, kom³ tso² hui⁵ pin¹ shue³ ni¹?

早晨, 先生, 咁早去邊處呢？

2 No where particular, to-day some people want me to help them to divide a property for them.

Mo₂ pin¹ shue³ hui³, kam¹ yat₄ yau₂ yan₁ iu³ ngoh₂ t'ung₁ k'ui₂ fan¹ ka¹ 冇邊處去, 今日有人要我同佢分家

3 What a peculiar job it is!

Kom² tsau₃ hai₃ ho² tak₄ pit₄ ke³ sz₃!

咁 就 係 好 特 別 嘅 事

4 Some people think it is peculiar, but I am always doing these things.

Yau₂ yan₁ kin³ hai₃ tak₄ pit₄, taan₃ ngoh₂ shi₁ shi₁ yau₂ kom² ke³ sz₃.

有 人 見 係 特 別, 但 我 時 時 有 咁 嘅 事

5 Is that so? There are all kinds of affairs (things) in the world.

Hai₃ me¹? Ngoh₂ tei₃ yan₁ chung² chung² sz₃ to¹ yau₂

係 咩？ 我 哋 人 種 種 事 都 有

6 In this case there is something peculiar.

Ni¹ kin₅ sz₃ yau₂ ti¹ tak₄ pit₄. 呢件事有啲特別

7 Why is it peculiar?

Yau₂ mat⁴ ye₂ tak₄ pit₄ ni¹? 有乜野特別呢

8 There are two brothers, one wants to change his style of dress, but the other does not. So they wish to live separately.

Leung₂ hing¹ tai₃ yat⁴ koh³ iu³ koi² chong¹, yat⁴ koh³ m₁ koi² tsau₃ iu³ fan¹ ka¹.

兩兄弟, 一个要改裝, 一个唔改, 就要分家

9 Is that so? So their point is not money. It is clothes.

Hai₃ me¹? tsau₃ m₁ kong² ho₁ tsz², hai₃ kong² shaam¹.

係 咩？ 就 唔 講 毫 子, 係 講 衫

10 They will discuss money, but at the beginnig it was not so.

To¹ hai₃ kong² ho₁ tsz², taan₃ hei² *t'au₁ m₁ hai₃.

都 係 講 毫 子, 但 起 頭 唔 係

第 四 十 六 課—Tai₃ sz³ shap₄ luk₄ foh³

1	照	Chiu¹—*According to, enlighten.*	**6**	雲	Wan₁—*Cloud.*
2	依	I¹—*According to, obey.*	**7**	怪	Kwaai³—*Strange, blame, uncanny.*
3	漸	*Tsim₃—*Gradually.*	**8**	雪	Suit₀ (suet₀)—*Ice, snow.*
4	風	Fung¹—*Wind, custom.*	**9**	然	In₁—*Thus, so, however, yes.*
5	吹	Ch'ui¹—*Blow.*	**10**	忽	Fat⁴—*Suddenly.*

1 照計今日咁好天,唔噲有雨落嚟 Chiu³ kai³ kam¹ yat₄ kom⁸ ho² t'in¹, in₁ ooi₂ yau₂ ue₂ lok₄ ke⁰
— According to to-day's weather, it will not rain.

2 我估照依你講係啱 Ngoh₂ koo² chiu³ i¹ nei₂ kong² hai₃ ngaam¹·
— I think what you say is right.

3 但係个天漸漸黑啲. Taan₁ hai₃ koh⁸ t'in¹ tsim₃ tsim₃ hak⁴ ti¹.
— But the sky is gradually becoming darker.

4 係有風打唔係呢. Hai₃ yau₂ fung¹ ta² m³ hai₃ ni¹?
— Is a typhoon coming?

5 係打風唔係,我就唔知 但係風吹落好多野 Hai₃ ta² fung¹ m₁ hai₃, ngoh₂ tsau₃ m₁ chi¹, taan₃ hai₃ fung¹ ch'ui¹ lok₄ ho² toh¹ ye₂.
— I do not know whether a typhoon is coming, the wind, however, has blown down many things.

6 我唔見有雲. Ngoh₂ m₁ kin³ yau₂ wan₁.
— I do not see that there are any clouds.

7 啲雲有時好奇怪. Ti¹ wan₁ yau₂ shi₁ ho² k'ei₁ kwaai³.
— The clouds sometimes are very peculiar.

8 落雪好好睇. Lok₄ suit₀ ho² ho² t'ai².
— When it snows it is very pretty.

9 今日我見唔自然. Kam¹ yat₄ ngoh₂ kin³ m₁ tsz₃ in₁.
— I do not feel well to-day.

10 點解忽然間天黑呢. Tim² kaai² fat⁴ in₁ kaan¹ t'in¹ hak⁴ ni₁?
— Why is the sky suddenly so overcast?

Suit₀ is written in place₀ of Suet lest people should read is as Su-et.

The Forty-sixth Exercise—(Conversation.)

1 To-day something has suddenly happened.

Kam[1] yat$_4$ yau$_2$ kin$_3$ sz$_3$ fat[4] in$_1$ faat$_0$ shaang[1] hei[2] lai$_1$.

今 日 有 件 事 忽 然 發 生 起 嚟

2 What is it ?

Yau$_2$ mat[4] ye$_2$ sz$_3$ ni[1] ? 有 乜 野 事 呢

3 You know the customs of China are constantly changing.

Nei$_2$ chi[1] ngoh$_2$ tei$_3$ Chung[1] kwok$_0$ yat$_4$ yat$_4$ koi[2] fung[1] hei[3] a[1] ? 你 知 我 哋 中 國 日 日 改 風 氣 吖

4 Yes, certainly ; they are gradually changing, there is no way of stopping the change.

Hai$_3$ a[1], tsim$_3$ *tsim$_3$ koi[2], *ting$_3$ la[1], mo$_2$ faat$_0$ tsz[2] m$_1$ koi[2]. 係 吖, 漸 漸 改 定 喇, 冇 法 子 唔 改

5 Why is there no way of stopping the change ?

Tim[2] kaai[2] mo$_2$ faat$_0$ tsz[2] ni[1] ? 點 解 冇 法 子 呢

6 (In Chinese the word "fung[1]" has two meanings; namely, customs and wind), you said wind, winds are constantly changing,

Nei$_2$ to[1] wa$_3$ fung[1], fung[1] shi$_1$ shi$_1$ to[1] pin[3] a[s]. 你 都 話 風, 風 時 時 都 變 呀 !

7 "Wind" is one thing, "Custom" is another.

Chui[1] fung[1] hai$_3$ yat[4] kin$_3$ sz$_3$, kwok$_0$ fung[1] tsau$_3$ m$_1$ t'ung$_1$. 吹 風 係 一 件 事, 國 風 就 唔 同

8 What is the difference ? In the atmosphere, the winds are constantly changing, of a country, the customs are also constantly changing.

Yau$_2$ mat[4] m$_1$ t'ung$_1$, t'in[1] fung[1] pin[s], kwok$_0$ fung[1] to[1] pin[3]. 有 乜 唔 同, 天 風 變, 國 風 都 變

9 What you say is right, in winter the air is sometimes as cold as ice.

Nei$_2$ kong[2] tak[4] yau$_2$ lei$_2$, t'in[1] laang$_2$ tsau$_3$ suit$_0$ kom[3] tung[3]. 你 講 得 有 理, 天 冷 就 雪 咁 凍

10 When the clouds rise, the rain will soon fall.

Hai$_3$, yau$_2$ wan$_1$ hei[2], tsau$_3$ yau$_2$ ue$_2$ lok$_4$ lok$_0$. 係, 有 雲 起, 就 有 雨 落 咯

THE FORTY SEVENTH LESSON

第 四 十 七 課—Tai₅ sz³ shap₄ ts'at⁴ foh³

1	石	Shek₄—*Stone*	6	拆 Ch'aak₀—*Demolish, tear down*
2	磚	Chuen¹—*Brick*	7	牆 Ts'eung₁—*Wall*
3	灰	Fooi¹—*Lime, mortar*	8	瓦 Nga₂—*Tiles, earthen ware*
4	泥	Nai₁—*Clay, earth*	9	漏 Lau₃—*Leak, forget*
5	土	T'o²—*Earth, ground*	10	窻 Ch'eung¹—*Windows*

1 山 上 啲 石 係 好 大 Shaan¹ sheung₃ ti¹ shek₄ hai₃ ho² taai₃.

2 有人起屋用石,有人用磚 Yau₂ yan₁ hei² uk⁴ yung₃ shek₄ yau₂ yan₁ yung₃ chuen¹

3 用磚要用灰嚟起 Yung₃ chuen¹ iu³ yung₃ fooi¹ lai₁ hei²

4 泥多灰少唔好 Nai₁ toh¹ fooi¹ shiu² m₁ ho²

5 呢處啲泥土唔係好 Ni¹ shue¹ ti¹ nai₁ t'o² m₁ hai₃ ho².

6 呢間屋要拆至得 Ni¹ kaan¹ uk⁴ iu³ ch'aak₀ chi³ tak⁴

7 係先拆牆唔係呢 Hai₃ sin¹ ch'aak₀ ts'eung₁ m₁ hai₃ ni¹?

8 先拆瓦後來至拆牆 Sin¹ ch'aak₀ nga₂ hau₃ loi₁ chi³ ch'aak₀ ts'eung₁

9 瓦爛屋就漏 Nga₂ laan₃ uk⁴ tsau₃ lau₃

10 窻門都要閂 Ch'eung¹ *moon₁ to¹ iu³ shaan¹

1 The rocks on the hills are very large.

2 Some people build houses with stones and some with bricks.

3 The bricks must be joined by mortar (lime).

4 *If too much earth and too little lime is used, the mortar is bad*

5 The earth here is not good.

6 This house must be demolished.

7 Are we to take down the walls first?

8 Take down the roof first and demolish the walls afterwards.

9 If the tiles are broken the roof leaks.

10 The windows must also be bolted.

The Forty-seventh Exercise—(Conversation.)

1 I am very busy to-day.

Kam¹ yat₄ ngoh₂ sz₃ toh¹. 今 日 我 事 多

2 Why, are you building a lot of houses ?

Mat⁴ ni¹ ? Hei² ho² toh¹ uk⁴ hai₃ m₁ hai₃ a¹ ?

乜 呢? 起 好 多 屋 係 唔 係 吖

3 Yes, I have to purchase stones, bricks, lime and tiles. Everything is difficult

Hai₃, maai₂ shek₄, maai₂ chuen¹, maai₂ fooi¹, maai₂ nga₂, yeung₃ yeung₃ mat₄ *kin₃ to¹ naan₁ tak⁴.

係, 買 石, 買 磚, 買 灰, 買 瓦, 樣 樣 物 件 都 難 得.

4 Have you to go about everywhere to look for materials.

Iu³ leung₂ t'au₁ tsau² hui³ wan² hai₃ m₁ hai₃ ni¹ ?

要 兩 頭 走 去 搵 係 唔 係 呢

5 Yes, I have to get some good clay, demolish the old walls and make new windows.

Hai₃, ting₃ la¹, chung₃ iu³ wan² ho² nai₁ t'o², ch'aak₀ kau₁ ts'eung₁ tso, san¹ ch'eung¹. 係 定 嘅, 重 要 搵 好 坭 土, 拆 舊 牆 做 新 窗.

6 I have told you that you are so old that you should not do so much work

Ngoh₂ to¹ wa₃ nei₂ kom³ lo₂ *taai₃, m₁ ho² tso₃ kom³ toh¹ sz₃. 我 都 話 你 咁 老 大, 唔 好 做 咁 多 事

7 If I do not do this, what shall I have to do ?

Ngoh₂ m₁ tso₃ ni¹ ti¹, tso₃ mat⁴ ye₂ ho² ni¹ ?

我 唔 做 呢 啲, 做 乜 野 好 呢

8 Sit down a while, do not be in such a hurry. Is it not good for an old man to talk on virtue.

Ts'oh₂ ha₂ a¹! m₁ ho² kom³ kap⁴, lo₂ yan₁ hui³ kong¹ to, tak⁴ m₁ ho² me¹ ? 坐 吓 吖, 唔 好 咁 急 老 人 去 講 道 德 唔 好 咩

9 What morality shall I talk about ? Do you think I am a Christian?

Kong² mat⁴ to₂ tak⁴, nei₂ koo² ngoh₂ hai₅ yap₄ kaau³ me¹? 講 乜 道 德, 你 估 我 係 入 教 咩.

10 Why is it not good to become a Christian. A Christian may always talk on virtue.

Tsau² yan₄ kaan³ yau₂ mat⁴ m₁ ho², hoh² i₂ shi₁ shi₁ kong² to₂ tak⁴. 就 入 教 有 乜 唔 好 可 以 時 時 講 道 德

11 I still want to earn money.

Ngoh₂ chung₃ iu³ wan² *ts'in₁. 我 重 要 搵 錢

12 Why do you want to earn money? It is useless to leave money to your children, your children are all grown up, and can make money

Wan² ts'in₁ tso, mat⁴ ye₂, pei² tsai² nui₂ mo₂ yung₃, nei₂ ke³ tsai² nui₂ koh³ koh³ to¹ taai₃, koh³ koh³ to¹ ooi₂ wan² ts'in₁ lok₀. 搵 錢 做 乜 野 俾 仔 女 冇 用 你 嘅 仔 女 个 个 都 大, 个 个 都 會 搵 錢 咯

THE FORTY-EIGHTH LESSON

第 四 十 八 課—Tai₃ sz³ shap₄ paat₀ foh³

1	夠	Kau³—*Enough.*
2	本	Poon²—*Root, origin, capital.*
3	位	Wai₃ or Wai²—*Seat, position.*
4	賍	Shit₄—*Lose.*
5	賺	Chaan₂—*Gain.*
6	肯	Hang²—*Consent.*
7	爭	Chaang¹—*Strive.*
8	執	Chap⁴—*Pick up.*
9	反	Faan²—*Back, oppose*
10	對	Tui³—*Opposite, a pair.*

1 做呢啲生意夠做唔夠做呢
'Tso₃ ni¹ ti¹ shaang¹ i³ kau³ tso₄ m₁ kau³ tso₃ ni¹?

1 Is this business a profitable one?

2 本錢多可以夠，本少就唔夠
Poon² tsin₁ toh² hoh² i₂ kau³, poon² shiu² tsau₃ m₁ kau³.

2 If we have enough capital it is profitable, with small capital it is not.

3 呢處地位好 Ni¹ shue³ tei₅ wai₃ ho² (a³).

3 This is a good position (for business).

4 好就好，但係做生意要賍本
Ho² tsau₃ ho⁴, taan₃ hai₃ tso₅ shaang¹ i⁴ iu³ shit₄ poon².

4 Although this is a good place yet we lose money.

5 我估你有錢賺 Ngoh₂ koo² nei₂ yau₂ ts'in₁ chaan₃.

5 I think you are making money.

6 工人肯做工就有錢賺唔肯做就冇工俾佢做. Kung¹ yan₁ hang² tso₃ kung₁ tsau₃ yau₂ "ts'in₁ chaan₃ m₁ hang² tso₃ tsau₃ mo₂ kung¹ pei² k'ui₂ tso₅.

6 If work-men are willing to work we can earn money, otherwise they will lose their job.

7 點解你同佢哋爭 'Tim² kaai² nei₂ t'ung₃ k'ui₂ tei₃ chaang¹.

7 Why do you quarrel with them.

8 佢哋樣樣都執我嘅
K'ui₂ tei₃ yeung₃ yeung₃ to¹ chap⁴ ngoh₂ ke³.

8 They pick quarrels with me in everything.

9 个啲人好反骨嘅 Koh² ti¹ yɔn₁ ho² faan² kwat⁴ ke³.

9 Those people are very quarrelsome.

10 時時都話反對東家 Shi₁ shi₁ to⁴ wa₃ faan² tui³ tung¹ ka¹.

10 They always talk about opposing their employers

The Forty-eighth Exercise—(Conversation.)

1 It is hard to carry on business.

Tso₃ shaang¹ i³ chan¹ hai₃ naan₁　做生意眞係難

2 Why do you say that?　Being so large a firm as you are, what difficulties have you got.

Tim² kaai² wa₃ naan₁, nei₂ kom³ taai₃ shaang¹ i³ yau₂ mat⁴ naan₁ shue³ ni¹?

點解話難, 你咁大生意, 有乜難處呢.

3 You say it is not hard, I am always thinking of making money.

Chung₂ wa₃ m₁ *naan₁, sheng₁ yat₄ iu³ hui³ wan² *ts'in₁

重話唔難, 成日要去搵錢

4 Why do you wish to raise money?

Wan² *ts'in₁ tso₅ mat⁴ ye₂?　搵錢做乜野.

5 The capital being insufficient is it not necessary for me to procure more money?

M₁ kau³ poon² m₁ hai₃ iu³ wan² me¹?

唔夠本唔係要搵咩.

6 Your business is so large, why do you still wish to procure more capital.

Nei₂ shaang¹ i³ kom³ taai₃, chung₂ wan² poon² ts'in₁ tso₃ mat⁴ ye₂?

你生意咁大, 重搵本錢做乜野.

7 I have to develop my business.

Iu³ tso₃ taai₃ ti¹ chi³ tak⁴ (a³)　要做大啲至得.

8 Do you wish to carry on business as big as the world?

Nei₂ seung² tso₃ t'in¹ has₃ kom³ taai₃ shaang¹ i³ me¹?

你想做天下咁大生意咩.

9 Why not?　only I fear I cannot achieve it.

Yau₂ mat⁴ m₁ seung², chi³ p'a³ tso, m₁ to³

有乜唔想至怕做唔到.

10 When carrying on so big a business, many people would oppose you, they would not be willing for you to earn so much money exclusively.

Tso₃ kom³ taai₃ p'a³ ho² toh¹ yan₁ faan² tui³ nei₃, k'ui₂ tei₃ m₁ hang² pei² nei₂ yat⁴ koh³ yan₁ chaan₃ kom³ toh¹

做咁大好多人反對你, 佢哋唔肯俾你一个人賺咁多

11 How could they hinder me?

Yau₂ mat⁴ m₁ pei² ni¹?　有乜唔俾呢

12 You see; So many people quarrel, affairs will change for the worse

Nei₂ t'aai² ha₃, toh¹ yan₁ chaang¹ chap⁴, tsau₂ pin³ tak⁴ m₁ ho²

你睇吓, 多人爭執, 就變得唔好.

Me¹ is a very common interrogative ending.

THE FORTY-NINTH LESSON

第 四 十 九 課—Tai₃ sz³ shap₄ kaau² foh³

1	收	Shau¹--*Receive, collect*	6	擔	Taam¹ or taan ̄—*Undertake, carry, a load*
2	租	Tso¹—*Rent*	7	保	Po²—*Protect, guarantee*
3	單	Taan¹—*Account, bill, receipt*	8	信	Sun³—*Letter, believe, faithful*
4	轉	Chuen²—*Revolve* Chuen³—*Turn, over*	9	欠	Him³—*To owe*
5	交	Kaau¹—*Intercourse, give, pay*	10	還	Waan₁—*Return, repay*

1 佢嚟問收乜野. K'ui₂ lai¹ man₃ shau¹ mat⁴ ye₂

What did they come to collect ?

2 佢嚟問收租. K'ui₂ lai₁ man₃ shau¹ tso¹.

They came to collect the rent.

3 我租佢嘅屋, 佢做屋主, 點解唔俾租單我. Ngoh₂ tso‧k'ui‧ke³ uk , k'ui₂ tso‧ uk chue², tim² kaai² m₁ pei² tso¹ taan¹ ngoh₂?

I rent his house, he is the landlord, why does he not give me the rent receipt ?

4 佢話你轉租過別人. K'ui₂ wa₃ nei₂ chuen² tso¹ kwoh³ pit₄ yan₁.

He says that you sublet to another person.

5 我个个月都有租交, 屋主不能打理我轉租過別人. Ngoh₂ koh³ koh‧uet₁ to¹ yau₂ tso¹ kaau¹, uk⁴ chue² pat⁴ nang₁ ta² lei₂ ngoh₂ chuen² tso¹ kwoh³ pit₄ yan₁.

I pay my rent every month. The landlord cannot interfere with if I sublet the house.

6 邊个同你擔租呢. Pin¹ koh³ t'ung₁ nei₂ taam¹ tso¹ ni¹?

Who guarantees the rent for you ?

7 冇人擔租嘅, 但係屋主想我搵人擔保. Mo₂ yan₁ taam¹ tso¹ ke³, taan hai‧ uk‧chue² seung² ngoh₂ wan² yan₁ taam¹ po².

Nobody guarantees the rent for me, but the landlord wants me to find a guarantor.

8 今日屋主寫擔保信嚟 問你幾時至交租 Kam¹ yat₄ uk⁴ chue² se² taam¹ po² sun³ lai₁, man₁ nei₂ kei² shi₁ chi₃ kaau¹ tso¹.

To-day the landlord sent you a registered letter asking you when you will pay the rent.

9 欠佢个半月租 使乜咁緊要吖 Him³ k'ui₂ koh³ poon² uet₁ tso¹ shai² mat¹ kom‧ kan² iu a¹.

I owe him one and a half month's rent, why need he be so pressing ?

10 你估我欠錢冇還咩. Nei₂ koo² ngoh₂ him³ ts'in₁ mo₂ waan₁ me¹.

Do you think that I will not pay my debts.

The Forty-ninth Exercise—(Conversation.)

1 It is very hard to collect rents.

Shau¹ tso¹ chan¹ hai₃ naan₁ lok₀ 收租真係難咯

2 Why is it hard, (to collect rents)?

Yau₂ mat⁴ ye₂ naan₁ ni¹? 有乜野難呢?

3 The landlord wants the rent, and the tenant has no money, what shall I do?

Uk⁴ chue²iu³ *ts'in₁, tso¹ uk⁴ ti¹ yan₁ mo₂ *ts'in₁, nei₂ wa₃ tim² tso₃ ho² ni¹? 屋主要錢,租屋的人冇錢,你話點做好呢?

4 You must ask him to find some one to guarantee his rent.

Iu³ k'ui₂ wan² yan₁ taam¹ po² chi° tak⁴ 要佢搵人担保至得.

5 The tenants do whatever they like. Some sublet the houses whilst some always pay the rents in arrear.

Koh² ti¹ tso¹ uk⁴ ke³ yan₁, mat⁴ ye₂ to¹ yau₂ tak⁴ tso₃, yau₂ ti¹ chuen² tso¹ kwoh³ yan₁, yau₂ ti¹ shi₁ shi₁ him³ tso¹.
個的租屋嘅人,乜野都有得做,有嘅轉租過人,有的時時欠租

6 If you make them pay the rents in advance you will have no more trouble.

Nei₂ iu³ k'ui₂ shi₁ shi₁ kaau¹ sheung₃ k'ei₁ tso¹, m₁ hai₃ tsau₃ mo₂ sz₃ lok₀? 你要佢時時交上期租,唔係就冇事咯

7 They will not do that. If I send them letters they refuse to receive them (letters) If I give them the accounts they have no money to settle them.

K'ui₂ m₁ hang² a³, kaau¹ sun³ k'ui₁ m₁ shau¹, kaau¹ taan¹ k'ui₂ mo₂ *ngan₁ 佢唔肯呀,交信佢唔收交單佢冇銀.

8 It will not do, when will they pay up the outstanding rents?

Kom' m₁ tso₁ tak⁴, k'ui₂ kei² *shi₁ chi³ waan₁ kau³ ti¹ kau₃ tso¹ ni¹? 咁唔做得,佢幾時至還夠的舊租呢.

9 Well, most of them will pay, but they will not pay when the rents are due.

Kom', yau₂ toh¹ sho³ to¹ hang² pei², pat⁴ kwoh³ hai₃ m₁ i' k'ei₁ 咁,有多數都肯俾,不過係唔依期.

10 This is better, or I would not stand it (any longer.)

Kom' tsau₃ ho² ti', m₁ hai, ngoh₂ yat⁴ teng₃ m₁ hang². 咁就好嘅,唔係,我一定唔肯.

THE FIFTIETH LESSON

第 五 十 課—Tai₃ ng₂ shap₄ foh³

1	富	Foo³—*Rich*	6	贏 Yeng₁—*Win*
2	窮	K'ung₁—*Poor, poverty*	7	輸 Shue¹—*Lose*
3	賭	To²—*Gamble*	8	求 K'au₁—*Seek, ask, pray*
4	害	Hoi₃—*Injure, harmful*	9	借 Tse³—*Lend, borrow*
5	呃	Ngaak⁴—*Deceive, cheat*	10	欵 Foon²—-*Funds, money*

1 一个人有好多錢就係富
Yat koh³ yan₁ yau₂ ho² toh¹ tsin₁ tsau₃ hai₃ foo³.

1 When a man has a great amount of money, then he is rich.

2 點解佢窮得咁緊要吖？
Tim² kaai² k'ui₂ k'ung₁ tak⁴ kom³ kan² iu³ a¹.

2 Why is he so extremely poor?

3 佢時時都賭，一有錢就賭 點得唔窮呢？ K'ui₂ shi₁ shi₁ to¹ to², yat⁴ yau₂ tsin₁ tsau₃ to², tim² tak⁴ m₁ k'ung₁ ni¹ ？

3 He always gambles, directly he has money he gambles, how can he avoid poverty.

4 賭錢真係害人咯. To² 'tsin₁ chan¹ hai₃ hoi₃ yan₁ lok₀

4 Gambling really is injurious to people.

5 賭錢多數係呃人嘅 To² tsin₁ toh¹ sho³ hai₃ ngaak⁴ yan₁ ke⁵.

5 Gambling is mostly cheating people.

6 佢昨日贏咗一千三百銀 K'ui₂ tsok₄ yat₄ yeng₁ choh² yat⁴ ts'in¹ saa·n¹ paak₀ ngan₁.

6 Yesterday he won 1300 dollars.

7 今日佢輸番一千七百銀 Kam¹ yat₄ k'ui₂ shue¹ faan¹ yat⁴ ts'in¹ ts'at⁴ paak₀ ngan₁.

7 To-day he lost 1700 dollars again.

8 有錢个時佢唔求人. Yau₂ *ts'in₁ koh² shi₁ k'ui₂ m₁ k'au₁ yan₁.

8 When he has money, he does not ask people (for it).

9 賭輸咗，佢唥嚟求我借錢 To² shue¹ choh², k'ui₂ ooi₂ lai₁ k'au₁ ngoh₂ tse³ *ts'in₁.⁴

9 When he loses he will come to me to borrow money.

10 佢欠人借款不少. K'ui₂ him³ yan₁ tse³ foon² pat⁴ shiu².

10 He owes a great deal of money that he has borrowed.

The Fiftieth Exercise—(Conversation.)

1 Why do some people like to gamble so much ?

Tin₁² kaai² yau₂ ti¹ yan₁ kom³ chung¹ i³ to² *ts'in₁ ni¹?

點 解 有 的 人 咁 中 意 賭 錢 呢?

2 Because they want to win money.

† Yan¹ wai₃ k'ui₂ seung² yeng₁ *ts'in₁

因 爲 佢 想 贏 錢

3 What if they cannot win ?

K'ui₂ yeng₁ m₁ to² tsau₃ tim² *yeung₁ ni¹ ?

佢 贏 唔 倒 就 點 樣 呢?

4 If they do not win, they lose.

Yeng₁ m₁ to² tsau₃ hai₃ shue¹ 贏 唔 倒 就 係 輸

5 If they lose a large amount, what then ?

Shue¹ tak⁴ toh¹ ooi₂ tim² *yeung₃ ni¹ ?

輸 得 多 嚹 點 樣 呢?

6 If they lose a lot they become poor.

Shue⁴ tak⁴ toh¹ ooi₂ k'ung₁ 輸 得 多 嚹 窮.

7 Well is not gambling a great evil ?

Kom² *yeung₃ to² *ts'in₁ m₁ hai₃ ho² taai₃ hoi₃ ke³ ?

咁 樣, 賭 錢 唔 係 好 大 害 嘅

8 Certainly it is a great evil.

Tsz₃ in₁ hai₃ ho² taai₃ hoi₃ 自 然 係 好 大 害.

9 He owes a lot of money to the gambling ship.

K'ui₂ him' hoi¹ to² ke³ yan₁ ho² toh¹ tse³ foon²

佢 欠 開 賭 嘅 人 好 多 借 款

10 I say that gambling is very injurious.

Ngoh₂ wa₃ to² *ts'in₁ hai₃ hoi₃ yan₁ ho² kan² iu³ a¹.

我 話 賭 錢 係 害 人 好 緊 要 吖.

† Because, see separate list. Yan¹ wai₃

112

THE FIFTY-FIRST LESSON

第 五 十 一 課—Tai₃ ng₂ shap₄ yat⁴ foh³

1	世	Shai³—*The world.*	6	俗	Tsuk₄—*Common.*
2	界	Kaai³—*Boundary, territory.*	7	省	Shaang²—*A province.* Sing²—*To examine, watch*
3	限	Haan₃—*Limit.*	8	城	*Shing₁—*A city.*
4	鄉	Heung¹—*Village, country.*	9	市	Shi₂—*A market.*
5	村	Ts'uen¹—*Village.*	10	店	Tim³—*A shop.*

1 自出世至到死叫做一世
Tsz₃ ch'ut⁴ shai³ chi³ to⁸ sz² kiu³ tso₃ yat⁴ shai⁵.

1 From the time of one's birth to one's death is called a generation.

2 世界有好多國. Shai³ kaai⁵ yau₂ ho² toh¹ kwok₀.

2 There are many countries in the world.

3 世界大國有限, 至多不過二三十个. Shai⁵ kaai³ taai₃ kwok₀ yau₂ haan₃, chi³ toh¹ pat⁴ kwoh³ i₃ saam¹ shap₄ koh³.

3 The large countries are not many, only 20 or 30.

4 有人住鄉間. Yau₂ yan₁ chue₃ heung¹ kaan¹.

4 Some people live in villages.

5 鄉間有人叫做鄉村. Heung¹ kaan¹ yau₂ yan₁ kiu³ tso₁ heung¹ ts'uen¹.

5 The country places are called villages.

6 各處鄉村有各處嘅風俗 Kok₀ shue³ heung¹ ts'uen¹ yau₂ kok₀ shue³ ke³ fung¹ tsuk₄.

6 There are different customs in different villages.

7 中國有二十幾省. Chung¹ kwok₀ yau₂ i₃ shap₄ kei² shaang².

7 There are more than twenty provinces in China.

8 每省都有省城. Mooi₂ shaang² to¹ yau₂ shaang² shing₁

8 There is a provincial city in each province.

9 大城多數有街市, 去街市買食物. Taai₃ shing₁ toh¹ sho⁵ yau₂ kaai³ shi₂, hui³ kaai¹ shi₂ maai₃ shik₁ mat₄.

9 In large cities there are mostly market places, people go to them to buy food.

10 喺城有好多酒店. Hai² shing₁ yau₂ ho² toh¹ tsau² tim³.

10 There are many wine shops in cities.

The Fifty-first Exercise—(On Customs.)

There are many countries in the world.

Shai^3 kaai^3 yau$_2$ ho^2 toh^1 kwok$_0$

世 界 有 好 多 國.

Each country has its boundary.

Kok$_0$ kwok$_0$ to^1 yau$_0$ kwok$_0$ kaai^3.

各 國 都 有 國 界.

In the nation there are villages.

Kwok$_0$ noi$_3$ yau$_2$ heung^1 ts'uen^1

國 內 有 鄉 村.

and markets

Yau$_2$ shing$_1$ shi$_2$

有 城 市

Sometimes the customs of villages,

Yau$_2$ shi$_1$ heung^1 ts'uen^1 ke^3 fung^1 tsuk$_4$

有 時 鄉 村 嘅 風 俗.

and those of the cities and markets,

T'ung$_1$ shing$_1$ shi$_2$ ke^3 fung^1 tsuk$_4$

同 城 市 嘅 風 俗

are very different,

yau$_2$ ho^2 taai$_3$ fan^1 pit$_4$

有 好 大 分 別

Once I went to Canton,

Ngoh$_2$ yau$_2$ yat^4 ooi$_1$ hui^3 shaang^2 shing$_1$

我 有 一 囘 去 省 城

and lived in a hotel,

hai^2 yat^4 kaan^1 tsau^2 tim^5 chue$_3$

喺 一 間 酒 店 住

I saw that in taking food

Ngoh$_2$ kin^3 k'ui$_2$ tei$_3$ shik$_4$ faan$_3$

我 見 佢 哋 食 飯

they did not use chopsticks,

m$_1$ hai$_3$ yung$_3$ faai^3 tsz^2

唔 係 用 快 子

But used knives and forks,

Taan$_3$ hai$_3$ yung$_3$ to^1 ch'a^1

但 係 用 刀 叉

and soup spoons,

to^1 yung$_3$ t'ong^4 kang^1

都 用 湯 羹

They were different from us in every way

Yeung$_3$ yeung$_1$ m$_1$ t'ung$_1$ ngoh$_2$ tei$_3$

樣 樣 唔 同 我 哋

It was very strange,

Chan^1 hai$_3$ k'ei$_1$ kwaai^3 lok$_0$

真 係 奇 怪 咯.

第 五 十 二 課—Tai₃ ng₂ shap₄ i₃ foh³

1	客	Haak₀—*A guest, customer*	6	煎	Tsin¹—*To fry*
2	望	Mong₃—*To hope*	7	廚	Ch'ue₁—*A cook, kitchen*
3	發	Faat₃—*To give out, send*	8	卽	Tsik⁴—*At once, now*
4	探	T'aam⁵—*To visit*	9	燴	Ooi₃—*Stew*
5	煮	Chue²—*To cook*	10	煲	Po¹—*Boil, (in a pot)*

1 唔係家內人，叫做客.
M₁ hai₃ ka¹ noi₃ yan₃, kiu³ tso₃ haak₀.

1 Those not of one's family are called visitors or guests.

2 佢望有好多錢睇. K'ui₂ mong₃ yau₂ ho² toh¹ ts'in₃ chaan₃

2 He hopes to make a lot of money.

3 明日出發，就發信請客
Ming₁ yat₄ ch'ut⁴ faat₀, tsau₃ faat₀ sun³ ts'eng² haak₀.

3 To-morrow he is going-away and so he is sending letters to invite guests.

4 後日喻有客嚟探我.
Hau₃ yat₄ ooi₂ yau₂ haak₀ lai₁ t'aam⁵ ngoh₂.

4 The day after to-morrow there will be guests coming to visit me.

5 係煮飯俾佢食唔係
Hai₃ chue² faan₃ pei² k'ui₂ shik₄ m₁ hai₃.

5 Will you cook rice for them (to eat).

6 飯一定有嘅 我想煎餅俾佢食.
F'aan₃ yat⁴ teng₃, yau₂ ke', ngoh₂ seung² tsin¹ peng² pei² k'ui₂ shik₄.

6 Yes, certainly they will have rice, I want to make cakes for them.

7 你个廚係好熱手 好燴煮野嘅
Nei₂ koh⁵ ch'ue₁ hai₃ ho² shuk₄ shau², ho² ooi₂ chue² ye₂ ke³.

7 Your cook is very experienced he is good at cooking things.

8 卽時叫起手，就有野食.
Tsik⁴ shi₁ kiu⁵ hei² shau², tsau₃ yau₂ ye₂ shik₄.

8 Directly you tell him he has things (ready) for eating.

9 佢燴雞第一好手勢.
K'ui₂ ooi₃ kai¹ tai₃ yat⁴ ho² shau² shai.

9 He is a first class man at stewing chickens,

10 係, 佢煲湯頂好手勢.
Hai₃, k'ui₂ po¹ t'ong¹ teng² ho² shau² shai₃.

10 Yes, he is very good at making soup.

The Fifty-second Exercise—(Conversation.)

1 Do you want to invite some guests?
Nei$_2$ hai. seung^2 ts'eng^2 haak$_0$ m$_1$ hai$_3$?
你 係 想 請 客 唔 係.

2 Yes, I am asking guests to-day.
Hai$_3$, ngoh$_2$ kam^1 yat$_4$ ts'eng^2 haak$_0$ 係,我今日請客.

3 Are they specially invited?
Hai$_1$ tak$_4$ pit$_4$ ts'eng^2 haak$_1$ m$_1$ hai$_1$?
係 特 別 請 客 唔 係.

4 No, it is just ordinary rice (meal).
M$_1$ hai$_3$, hai$_3$ shik$_4$ pin$_3$ *faan$_3$ ke^3
唔 係, 係 食 便 飯 嘅.

5 How do you invite them?
Nei$_1$ tim^2 *yeung$_3$ ts'eng^2 a$^.$? 你 點 樣 請 呀.

6 If I meet them I ask them, if not I send letters to invite them.
Ngoh$_2$ kin^3 to^2 tsau$_1$ kiu^3, m$_1$ kin^3 tsau$_3$ faat$_1$ sun^3 hui^3 ts'eng^2 我 見 倒 就 叫,唔 見 就 發 信 去 請.

7 What are you giving them to eat?
Yau$_2$ mat^4 ye$_2$ pei^2 k'ui$_2$ shik$_4$ ni^1?
有 乜 野 俾 佢 食 呢.

8 We will stew a fowl, roast some beef and have white cabbage flowers.
Yau$_2$ ooi$_3$ kai^1, shiu^1 ngau$_1$ yuk$_3$, paak$_0$ ts'oi^3 sam^1
有 燴 雞, 燒 牛 肉, 白 菜 心.

9 Will you use chopsticks or knives and forks?
Yung$_3$ faai^3 tsz^2, ting$_.$ to^1 ch'a^1 ni^1?
用 快 子, 定 刀 叉 呢.

10 We are not asking them to a meal, (foreign style), we will cut up the meat and use chopsticks to eat with.
Shik$_4$ faan$_3$ m$_1$ hai$_3$ tso$_.$ ts'aan^1, yung$_3$ faai^3 tsz^2 shik$_4$ faan$_3$, tsit$_0$ sai^3 ti^1 yuk$_4$
食 飯 唔 係 做 餐,用 快 子 食 飯 切 細 的 肉.

THE FIFTY-THIRD LESSON

第 五 十 三 課—Tai₅ ng₂ shap₁ saam¹ foh⁵

1	整	Ching²—*Make, do.*	**6**	在	Tsoi₃—*To be in.*
2	平	P'ing₁—*Even.* P'eng₁—*Cheap.*	**7**	現	In₃—*Present.*
3	價	Ka³—*Price.*	**8**	金	Kam¹—*Gold.*
4	跌	Tit₀—*Full.*	**9**	低	Tai¹—*Low.*
5	值	Chik₄—*Value, worth*	**10**	萬	Maan₃—*10,000.*

1 近來整得各樣貨都貴
Kan₅ loi₁ ching² tak¹ kok₀ yeung₃ foh⁵ to¹ kwai².

1 Lately the price of all goods has become very expensive.

2 想買平野真係幾難
Seung² maai₂ p'eng₁ ye₂ chan¹ hai₃ kei² naan₁.

2 It is very difficult to buy cheap things.

3 成本貴, 價錢自然高.
Shing₁ poon² kwai³ ka⁵ ts'in₁ tsz₈ in₁ ko¹.

3 If the capital cost is dear the price is certain to be high.

4 樣樣野起價 淨係麥粉跌價.
Yeung₃ yeung₅ ye₂ hei² ka₃, tsing₃ hai₀ mak₄ fan² tit₀ ka³.

4 Everything has risen in price, only oatmeal has dropped (in price).

5 一箱麥粉值六个半銀錢. Yat⁴ seung¹ mak₄ fan² chik₄ luk₄ koh³ poon³ ngan₁ ts'in₁.

5 One case of oatmeal is worth $6.50.

6 在別處買可以平的.
Tsoi₃ pit₄ shue³ maai₂ hoh² i, p'eng₁ ti¹.

6 It may be bought cheaped in another place.

7 現在洋酒漸漸貴. In₃ tsoi₃ yeung₁ tsau² tsim₅ tsim₅ kwai³.

7 Now foreign wine is gradually becoming dearer.

8 金價一日日高. Kam¹ ka³ yat⁴ *yat₄ yat₄ ko¹

8 The price of gold is constantly rising.

9 金價高銀價一定低.
Kam¹ ka² ko³ ngan₁ ka⁵ yat⁴ ting₅ tai¹.

9 If gold rises in price the price of silver is certain to fall.

10 呢啲貨值多過三萬銀, 有要多你嘅 Ni¹ ti¹ foh³ chik₄ toh¹ kwoh³ saam¹ maan₃ ngan₁ mo₀ iu⁵ toh¹ nei₂ ke⁵.

10 These goods are worth more than $30,000 I am not asking you too much.

The Fifty-third Exercise—(Conversation.)

1 What is called (meant by) the current price? (rate for the day).

Mat^4 ye, kiu^3 tso, shi, ka^3 ni^1 ? 乜野叫做時價呢.

2 The current price cannot be definitely settled. If it is cheap, it is cheap; if dear, dear, that is called the current price.

Shi, ka^3 hai, pat^4 nang, teng, shat, kei^2 toh^1 ka^3 ts'in, taan, hai, p'eng, tsau, p'eng, kwai^3 tsau, kwai^3, kom^2 tsau, kiu^8 tso, shi, ka^8

時價係不能定寶幾多價錢,但係平就平,貴就貴,咁就叫做時價

3 Is the current price for business the value of gold.

Kam^1 ka' hai, shi, ka^3 maai, maai, m, hai,

金 價 係 時 價 買 寶 唔 係.

4 Yes, dealings in silver and gold are certainly at the rate of the day, because there is no certainty about rise and fall.

Hai,, kam^1 ngau, yat^4 teng, yau, shi, ka^3 maai, maai, yan^1 wai, hei^2 tit, mo, teng,

係金銀一定有時價,買賣,因為起跌冇定

5 What is the present price of gold?

In, tsoi, kam' maai, mat^4 ye, ka^3 ni^1 ?

現 在 金 寶 乜 野 價 呢

6 I have not bought for a long time, I think the price is the same as before.

Ngoh, ho^2 noi, mo, maai,. ngoh, koo^2 chiu^3 kau, shi, yat^4 yeung, 我好耐冇買,我估照舊時一樣.

7 Your ideas are wrong, do you know whether the present price of gold is high or low?

Nei, koo^2 ts'oh^3 choh^2 lok, nei, chi^1 in, tsoi, kam^1 ka^8 ko^1 pei, tai^1 ni^1 ?

你估錯咖咯,你知現在金價高嗎低呢.

8 Really I do not know whether it is high or low.

Kam^1 ka^3 ko^1 tai', ngoh, shat, tsoi, m, chi^1

金 價 高 低, 我 寶 在 唔 知.

9 How much is a 8,9 large gold coin (American $20.00)?

Yat^4 koh^5 paat, kau^2 taai, kam^1, chik, tak^4 kei^2 toh^1 *ngan, ni^1 ? 一个八九大金值得幾多銀呢.

10 One one-two English gold piece (sovereign) is worth more than 10 dollars, one 8.9 large coin is at least worth several tens of dollars.

Yat^4 koh^3 yat^4 i, ying^1 kam^1 to^1 chik, tak^4 shap, kei^2 koh^3 ngan, *ts'in,, yat^4 koh^6 paat, kau^2 taai, kam^1, chi^3 shiu^2 chik, kei^2 shap, koh^8 ngan, *ts'in,.

一个一二英金都值得十幾个銀錢,一个八九大金,至少值幾十个銀錢.

THE FIFTY-FOURTH LESSON

第 五 十 四 課—Tai$_3$ ng$_2$ shap$_4$ sz^s foh^3

1	斟	Cham^1—*Pour out, discuss*		6	賬	Cheung^3— *Accounts*
2	着	Cheuk$_4$—*Right,* Cheuk$_0$—*Used for to wear*		7	幫	Pong^1—*Help, a shipment*
3	佣	Yung^2— *Commission*		8	寄	Kei^s—*Send*
4	減	Kaam^2—*Reduce, subtract*		9	再	Tsoi^3—*Again, further*
5	加	Ka^1—*Add, increase*		10	放	Fong^3—*Release*

1 你同佢斟乜野. Nei$_2$ t'ung$_1$ k'ui$_2$ cham^1 mat^4 ye$_2$?

1 What are you discussing with him?

2 我同佢斟着買啲洋貨. Ngoh$_2$ t'ung$_1$ k'ui$_2$ cham^1 cheuk$_1$ maai$_1$ ti^1 yeung$_1$ foh$^?$.

2 I am discussing the purchase of some foreign goods.

3 同你賣洋貨, 你俾幾多佣呢. T'ung$_1$ nei$_2$ maai$_1$ yeung$_1$ foh^3, nei$_2$ pei^2 kei^2 toh^1 yung^2 ni^1?

3 If I sell goods for you, what commission do you give?

4 舊時佢要佣太多 但係現在我想減佣 Kau$_3$ shi$_1$ k'ui$_2$ iu^3 yung^2 t'aai^1 toh^1, taan$_3$ hai$_1$ in$_s$ tsoi$_3$ ngoh$_2$ seung^2 kaam^2 yung^2

4 Formerly he wanted too much commission, but now I want to reduce the commission.

5 咁樣嘅價錢我唔可以加多 Kom^2 yeung$_s$ ke^s ka^3 ts'in$_1$ ngoh$_2$ m$_1$ hoh^2 i$_s$ ka^1 toh^1.

5 At such a price I cannot increase.

6 舊賬你都未結 呢回要現銀至得 Kau$_3$ cheung^3 nei$_2$ to^1 mei$_s$ kit$_3$, ni^1 ooi$_1$ iu^3 in$_1$ ngan$_1$ chi^3 tak^4.

6 You have not yet settled the old account, this time we must deal in cash.

7 有幫乜野貨到呢. Yau$_2$ pong^1 mat^4 ye$_2$ foh^3 to^3 ni^1?

7 What shipment of goods has arrived.

8 有一大幫牛皮 由英國寄嚟. Yau$_2$ yat^1 taai$_s$ pong^1 ngau$_1$ p'ei$_1$ yau$_1$ ying^1 kwok$_1$ kei^3 lai$_1$.

8 There is a large consignment of leather sent from England.

9 我寫信去牛皮公司 叫佢再寄啲貨嚟 Ngoh$_2$ ss^2 sun^3 hui^4 ngau$_1$ p'ei$_1$ kung^1 sz^1, kiu^3 k'ui$_2$ tsoi^3 kei^3 ti^1 foh^3 lai$_1$.

9 I have sent a letter to the leather (company) telling them to send more goods.

10 今日放假 明日至可以起貨. Kam^1 yat$_4$ fong^s ka^3, meng$_1$ yat$_4$ chi^s hoh^2 i$_2$ hei^2 foh^3.

10 To-day is a holiday, we cannot get the goods until to-morrow.

The Fifty-fourth Exercise—(On Making Money.)

1 One day there was a shipment of goods, sent from America.

Yat⁴ yat₄ yau₂ yat⁴ pong¹ foh⁵, hai² mei₂ kwok₀ kei³ lai₁

一 日 有 一 帮 貨，喺 美 國 寄 嚟.

2 He had no money to buy with, he went to a money lender to borrow in advance.

K'ui₂ mo₂ *ts'in₁ maai₂, hui² t'ung₁ yat⁴ koh³ fong³ cheung³ yan₁ tse³ chuen² sin¹

佢 冇 錢 買，去 同 一 个 放 賬 人 借 轉 先.

3 The two discussed it a long time, when the matter was arranged, he used all the borrowed money to buy goods.

Leung₂ ka¹ cham¹ cheuk₀ ho² noi₃, shing₁ sz₃ hau₃, k'ui₂ tseung¹ ti¹ tse' foon² hui³ maai₁ saai' foh³

兩 家 斟 着 好 耐，成 事 後，佢 將 啲 借 款 去 買 嘥 貨.

4 And made a lot of money. He used the money to repay people, and was free from debt.

Chaan₃ ho² toh¹ *ts'in₁, tseung¹ ti¹ *ts'in₁ waan₁ faan¹ pei² yan₁, mo₂ him³ yan₁ *ts'in₁

賺 好 多 錢，將 啲 錢 還 番 俾 人，冇 欠 人 錢.

5 His business prospered continually, his capital increased and did not diminish, and afterwards he became a rich man.

K'ui₂ ke³ shaang¹ i³ yat⁴ yat₄ yat₄ ho², poon² ts'in₁ yau₂ ka² mo₂ kaam², hau₃ loi₁ tso₃ yat⁴ koh³ yau₂ *ts'in₁ lo²

佢 嘅 生 意 一 日 日 好，本 錢 有 加 冇 減，後 來 做 一 个 有 錢 佬.

香港・澳門雙城成長經典

120

THE FIFTY-FIFTH LESSON

第 五 十 五 課—Tai₃ ng₂ shap₄ ng₂ foh³

1	舖	*P'o¹—A shop
2	搬	Poon¹—To remove, move
3	封	Fung¹—Close, seal up (classifier for letter)
4	埋	Maai₁—Near, come to (wharf) close
5	號	Ho₃—A number or name (of shop etc.)
6	回	Ooi₁—Return, back, one time
7	牌	P'aai₁—A signboard notice, dominoes
8	招	Chiu¹—To call, invite, summon
9	記	Kei³—Record, remember, a sign
10	址	Chi²—Address, basis, foundation

1 个間賣野嘅有人叫舖頭.
Koh² kaan¹ maai₃ ye₂ ke³ yau₂ yan₁ kiu³ p'o³ t'au₁.

A shop in which things are sold is called by some people a shop (p'o t'au).

2 有時屋主要屋客搬舖
Yau₂ shi₁ uk⁴ chue² iu³ uk⁴ haak₀ poon¹ p'o³.

Sometimes a landlord requires his tenant to remove.

3 欠租屋主嗌封舖. Him³ tso¹ uk⁴ chue² ooi₂ fung¹ p'o³.

If rent is owing the landlord will close the shop.

4 朝早个間舖閂埋門.
Chiu¹ tso² koh² kaan¹ p'o³ shaan¹ maai₁ moon₁.

In the early morning the shop door is closed.

5 呢間舖幾多號呢. Ni¹ kaan¹ p'o³ kei² toh¹ ho₃ ni¹?

What is the number of this shop?

6 个間舖我去過一回.
Koh⁴ kaan¹ p'o³ ngoh₂ hui³ kwoh³ yat⁴ ooi₁.

I have been to that shop once.

7 佢間舖幾多號門牌呢?
K'ui₂ kaan¹ p'o³ kei² toh¹ ho₃ moon₁ p'aai₁ ni¹?

What is the number of his shop?

8 我唔知幾多號門牌 但係我知佢嘅招牌名 Ngoh₂ m₁ chi¹ kei² toh¹ ho₃ moon₁ p'aai₁, taan₃ hai₃ ngoh₂ chi¹ k'ui₂ ke³ chiu¹ p'aai₁ meng₁.

I do not know his number (shop) but I know his sign (board) (shop name).

9 你記得佢嘅電話幾多號唔呢 Nei₂ kei³ tak⁴ k'ui₂ ke³ tin° wa₃ kei² toh¹ ho₃ m₁ ni¹?

Can you remember his telephone number?

10 唔記得 我不過記得佢嘅住址 M₁ kei³ tak⁴, ngoh₂ pat⁴ kwoh³ kei³ tak⁴ k'ui₂ ke³ chue₃ chi².

I cannot remember it. I can only remember his address. (residence).

The Fifty-fifth Exercise—(Conversation.)

1 Do you know where he has moved to ?

Nei₂ chi¹ k'ui₂ poon¹ hui³ pin¹ shue³ m₁ chi¹ ni¹ ?

你 知 佢 搬 去 邊 處 唔 知 呢?

2 I know he has moved to that street, but do not know the number.

Ngoh₂ chi¹ k'ui₂ poon¹ hui³ koh² t'iu₁ kaai¹, taan₃ m₁ chi¹ tai₁ kei² ho₁ moon₁ p'aai₁

我知佢搬去個條街,但唔知第幾號門牌.

3 Is it not the second door on the left after you enter the street ?

Yap₄ hui³ koh² t'iu₁ kaai¹, chuen² tsoh² pin₃ tai₃ i₃ kaan¹ hai₃ m₁ hai₃ a¹ ?

入去個條街,轉左便第二間係唔係吖.

4 I do not remember exactly. Once I sent a letter but it was returned, not delivered.

Ngoh₂ m₁ kei² tak⁴ chan¹, yau₂ yat⁴ ooi₁ ngoh₂ kei³ yat⁴ fung¹ sun³ hui³, kei³ m₁ to³, ta² ooi₁ t'au₁

我唔記得眞,有一回我寄一封信去,寄唔到,打回頭

5 Has he a signboard ? (lit. I do not know whether he has a signboard)

M₁ chi¹ k'ui₂ yau₂ chiu¹ p'aai₁ mo₂ ni¹ ?

唔 知 佢 有 招 牌 冇 呢.

6 He has a signboard, on which is written Faat Kei Ho.

Yau₂ chiu¹ p'aai₁, se² chue₃ faat₀ kei³ ho₃ saam¹ koh³ tsz₃

有 招 牌, 寫 住 發 記 號 三 个 字.

7 Now it is after 9 o'clock, I do not know what time he closes his shop.

In₃ tsoi₃ kau² tim² kei² chung¹, m₁ chi¹ k'ui₂ kei² toh¹ tim² chung¹ maai₁ p'o³ ni¹ ?

現在九點幾鐘,唔知佢幾多點鐘埋舖呢.

8 I think he will be closing soon.

Ngoh₂ koo² tsau₃ maai₁ p'o³ lok꜀. 我 估 就 埋 舖 咯

9 If you know his address, can you tell me ?

Nei₂ chi¹ shat₄ k'ui₂ ke³ tei₃ chi², wa₃ ngoh₂ chi¹ tak⁴ m₁ tak⁴ ni¹? 你知實佢嘅地址,話我知得唔得呢.

10 Yes, if I knew it I would tell you.

Tak⁴, ngoh₂ chi¹ ngoh₂ wa₃ nei₂ t'eng¹

得, 我 知 我 話 你 聽.

THE FIFTY-SIXTH LESSON

第五十六課—Tai₃ ng₂ shap₄ luk₄ foh³

1 和	Woh₁—*Harmony, peace*	**6** 失	Shat⁴—*Lost, lose.*
2 順	Shun₃—*Accord with, obey, yield.*	**7** 取	Ts'ui²—*To take.*
3 聯	Luen₁—*Unite, to sew.*	**8** 銷	Siu¹—*Finish, melt, cancel.*
4 報	Po³—*Report, A newspaper*	**9** 簽	Ts'im¹—*To sign (name).*
5 告	Ko³—*Inform, accuse.*	**10** 約	Yeuk₀—*An agreement, treaty.*

1 世界各國每每有事執後來和好
Shai³ kaai³ kok₀ kwok₀ mooi₂ mooi₂ yau₂ chaang¹ chap⁴, hau₃ loi₁ woh₁ ho²

1 All the nations of the world from time to time have disputes, afterwards they make peace.

2 順道理 各國可以合作.
Shun₃ to₃ lei₂ kok₀ kwok₀ hoh² i₂ hop₄ tsok₀

2 If they work in accordance with right principles they can work together.

3 有時兩國聯合做好多歡喜嘅事
Yau₂ shi₁ leung₂ kwok₀ luen₁ hop₄ tso₃ ho² toh¹ foon¹ hei² ke³ sz₃

3 Some times two countries unite and do many pleasant things.

4 一和後,就報知各國.
Yat⁴ woh₁ hau₃, tsau₃ po³ chi¹ kok₀ kwok₀

4 Directly they make peace, they report it to all the nations.

5 報知各國, 係用一張報告
Po³ chi¹ kok₀ kwok₀, hai₃ yung¹ yat⁴ cheung¹ po³ ko³

5 They inform the countries by means of a proclamation (memorandum.)

6 失和嘅事,害世界好多
Shat⁴ woh₁ ke³ sz₃, hoi₃ shai³ kaai¹ ho² toh¹

6 Breaches of the peace are very injurious to the world.

7 有時講和一國要取第二國嘅地
Yau₂ shi₁ kong² woh₁, yat⁴ kwok₀ iu² ts'ui² tai₃ i₃ kwok₀ ke³ tei₃

7 Sometimes when they discuss peace, one country wants to take territory from the other country.

8 但係友國要取銷以前不和嘅事
Taan₃ hai₃ yau₂ kwok₀ iu² ts'u² siu¹ i₂ ts'in₁ pat⁴ woh₁ ke³ sz₃

8 But friendly nations must annul former matters of disharmony.

9 兩家講和要簽字.
Leung₂ ka¹ kong² woh₁ iu² ts'im¹ tsz₃

9 The two parties having arranged peace must sign (an agreement)

10 兩國講和簽字, 叫做簽立和約
Leung₂ kwok₀ kong² woh₁ ts'im¹ tsz₃, kiu³ tso₂ ts'im¹ laap₄ woh₁ yeuk₀

10 When they sign a paper after making peace, it is called a Treaty of peace:—

The Fifty-sixth Exercise—(On Harmony.)

1 Breaking the peace, is a very disagreeable affair, we must always be at peace.

Shat^4 woh$_1$ ke^3 sz$_3$ hai$_3$ ho^2 fai^3 sz$_3$ ke^3, shi$_1$ shi$_1$ to^1 hai$_3$ iu^3 woh$_1$ ho^2 失和嘅事，係好費事嘅，時時都係要和好

2 All should unite, yesterday I bought a newspaper..

Taai$_3$ ka^1 luen$_1$ hop$_4$ chi^3 tak^4, tsok$_4$ yat$_4$ ngoh$_2$ maai$_2$ choh^2 yat^4 cheung^1 po^3 chi^2

大家聯合至得，昨日我買咗一張報紙，

3 That paper, said that there were two brothers, the younger accused the elder saying that the elder cheated him in the family property.

Koh^2 cheung^1 po^3 chi^2, maai$_3$ yau$_2$ leung$_2$ hing^1 tai$_3$ koh^3 sai^3 lo^2 ko^3 taai$_3$ lo^2, wa$_3$ taai$_3$ lo^2 ngaak^4 k'ui$_2$ shan^1 ka^1

个張報紙，賣有兩兄弟，个細佬告大佬，話大佬呃佢身家

4 His friend seeing that it did not look nice, told him not to do so, but to cancel the matter.

K'ui$_2$ ke^3 p'ang$_1$ yau$_2$ t'ai^2 kin^3 m$_1$ kwoh^3 tak^4 ngaan$_2$, kiu^3 k'ui$_2$ m$_1$ ho^2 kom^2 tso$_3$, iu^3 tseung^1 ni^1 kin$_3$ sz$_3$ ts'ui^2 siu^1

佢嘅朋友睇見唔過得眼，叫佢唔好咁做，要將呢件事取銷.

5 If not it would be a disgrace, and people would look down on them.

M$_1$ hai$_3$ ooi$_2$ shat^4 lai$_2$ yan$_1$, pei^2 ngoi$_3$ yan$_1$ t'aai^2 siu^2

唔係噲失禮人，俾外人睇小.

6 The younger brother thought it over, felt it was true, and the trouble ended.

Koh^3 sai^3 lo^2 seung^2 kwoh^3, kok$_0$ tak^4 hai$_3$ chan^1, tsoi$_3$ hau$_3$ mo$_2$ sz$_3$

个細佬想過，覺得係真，在後冇事.

THE FIFTY-SEVENTH LESSON

第 五 十 七 課—Tai₃ ng₂ shap₄ ts'at⁴ foh³

1	益	Yik⁴—*Benefit*
2	利	Lei₃—*Profit, interest*
3	息	Sik⁴—*Interest, rest*
4	派	P'aai³—*To give out, pay*
5	清	Ts'ing¹—*Clear, close account*
6	進	Tsun³—*Proceed, receipts*
7	支	Chi¹—*Pay out, expenditure*
8	存	Ts'uen₁—*Balance, remaining*
9	共	Kung₃—*With, together, all*
10	票	Piu¹—*A ticket, document, a tender* P'iu³—*A warrant*

1 讀書好有益. Tuk₄ shue¹ ho² yau₂ yik⁴

    Reading books is very beneficial.

2 做生意有乜利益呢. Tso shaang¹ i⁵ yau₂ mat¹ lei₃ yik⁴ ni¹?

    What is the benefit of doing business.

3 生意有錢賺, 就有利息分. Shaang¹ i⁵ yau₂ ts'in₁ chaan₃, tsau₃ yau₂ lei₃ sik⁴ fan¹.

    If money is made in the business then interest is paid (on one's capital).

4 呢間公司一年派幾多利息呢. Ni¹ kaan¹ kung¹ sz¹ yat⁴ nin₁ p'aai³ kei² toh¹ lei₃ sik⁴ ni¹?

    What interest does this company pay in a year.

5 有年派二分 有年派三分除清皮費至派. Yat₂ nin₁ p'aai³ i₃ fan¹, yau₂ nin₁ p'aai³ saam¹ fan¹ ch'ui₁ ts'ing¹ p'ei₁ fai³ chi³ p'aai³.

    Some years it gives 2%, if business is good it pays 3%, it is paid after deducting expenses.

6 舊年成年進款大約有幾多呢. Kau₃ nin₁ shing₁ nin₁ tsun³ foon² taai₁ yeuk₃ yau₂ kei² toh¹ ni¹?

    What was the total income last year? (approximately).

7 今日你有支銀俾佢冇. Kam¹ yat₄ nei₂ yau₂ chi¹ ngan₁ pei² k'ui₂ mo₂?

    Have you paid him any money to-day?

8 除支外實存現銀九萬圓 Ch'ui₁ chi¹ ngoi₃ shat₄ ts'uen₁ in₃ ngan₁ kau² maan₃ uen₁.

    After deducting expenditure, the actual balance is $90.000.

9 合共有好多現銀存. Hop₄ kung₃ yau₂ ho² toh¹ in₃ ngan₁ ts'uen₁.

    Altogether there is a large cash balance.

10 佢係收銀人 出入多 買長行票係好啦. K'ui₂ hai₃ shau¹ ngan₁ yan₁ ch'ut¹ yap₄ toh¹, maai₂ ch'eung₁ hang₁ p'iu³ hai₃ ho² ti¹.

    He is a collector he goes about a great deal it is better to buy a season ticket.

The Fifty-seventh Exercise—(On Business.)

1   A friend, and I opened a food shop, since we started, I have left everything in his care.

> Ngoh₂ t'ung₁ yat⁴ koh³ p'ang₁ yau₂, tso₃ yat⁴ kaan¹ shik₄ mat₄ *p'o³, tsz₃ hoi¹ cheung¹ i₂ loi₁, ngoh₂ kaan¹ saai³ kwoh⁵ k'ui₂ ta² lei₂

> 我同一个朋友，做一間食物舖自開張以來，我交過嘅佢打理

2   Every year there was a profit. During the last year or two, nominally there was a profit, but no interest was paid on capital.

> Nin₁ nin₁ to¹ yau₂ *ts'in₁ chaan₃, kan₃ ni¹ yat⁴ leung₂ nin₁ wa₃ *meng₁ yau₂ *ts'in₁ chaan₃, taan₃ hai₃ mo₂ lo₂ poon² sik⁴ p'aai³

> 年年都有錢聽，近呢一兩年話名有錢聽，但係冇老本息派

3   I asked him about the accounts, he was unable to tell me. I asked him more fully.

> Ngoh₂ man₃ k'ui₂ tsun³ chi¹ sho³, k'ui₂ mo₂ kai³ hoh² i₂ wa₃ ch'ut⁴, ngoh₂ tsoi³ man₃ chan¹ k'ui₂

> 我問佢進支數，佢冇計可以話出，我再問真佢

4   And he said there is not a cash left, I asked him where he had taken all the money.

> K'ui₂ wa₈ yat⁴ koh³ ts'in₁ to¹ mo₂ tak⁴ ts'uen₁, ngoh₂ man₃ k'ui₂ ning¹ saai³ ti¹ *ts'in₁ hui₃ pin¹ shue⁵

> 佢話一个錢都冇得存，我問佢摔哂啲錢去邊處

5   He said I have lost it. Seeing that it was useless to go on, I divided up with him.

> K'ui₂ wa₃ shue¹ choh², ngoh₂ kin³ kom² *yeung₃, tsoi³ tso₃ to¹ hai₃ mo₂ yik⁴, shoh² i₂ t'ung₁ k'ui₂ ch'aak₀ sho³

> 佢話輸嘅，我見咁樣，再做都係冇益，所以同佢拆數

6   And apart from the expenses made $500.

> Ch'ui₁ ts'ing¹ p'ei₂ fai³, kung₃ chaan₃ tak⁴ ng₂ paak₀ ngan₁

> 除清皮費，共聽得五百銀.

7   But he has no cash to give me, he wrote an I. O. U. promising to pay me in full at the end of this year.

> Taan₃ hai₃ k'ui₂ mo₂ in₄ *ts'in₁ pei² ngoh₂, se² faan¹ yat⁴ t'iu₁ him³ taan⁴, haan₃ i₂ kam¹ *nin₁ nin₁ mei₂ waan₁ ts'ing¹

> 但係佢冇現錢俾我，寫番一條欠單，限以今年年尾還清

THE FIFTY-EIGHTH LESSON

第 五 十 八 課—Tai₃ ng₂ shap₄ paat₀ foh³

1	民	Man₁—People	6	納	Naap₁—To pay, receive
2	港	Kong²—A port, Hong Kong	7	稅	Shui⁷—Customs, duty
3	會	Ui₃—A meeting, society	8	關	Kwaan¹—Customs
4	堂	T'ong₁—A hall, guild	9	法	Faat₀—A law, method
5	接	Tsip₀—To receive	10	例	Lai₃—An ordinance

1 一國嘅人叫做國民.
Yat⁴ kwok₀ ke⁷ yan₁ kiu⁷ tso₃ kwok₀ man₁.

1 The people of a country are called citizens.

2 香港好多中國人做生意
Heung¹ kong² ho⁷ toh¹ chung¹ kwok₀ yan₁ tso₃ shaang¹ i³.

2 Many Chinese do business in Hongkong.

3 民國有國會. Man₁ kwok₀ yau₂ kwok₀ *ui₃.

3 A Republic has a Council (or Senate).

4 香港教會有會堂 名叫禮拜堂.
Heung¹ kong² kaau³ ui₃ yau₂ ui₃ t'ong₁, ming₁ kiu³ lai₂ paai³ t'ong₁.

4 Hongkong Churches have meeting places, also called Houses of worship.

5 教會接收人要問心事.
Kaau³ ui₃ tsip₀ shau¹ yan₁ iu⁷ man₃ sam¹ sz₃.

5 When a Church receives a member, it requires to ask his views.

6 交息銀係納息. Kaau¹ sik⁴ ngan₁ hai₃ naap₄ sik⁴.

6 Handing over interest is paying interest

7 貨物要納稅. Foh³ mat₄ iu³ naap₄ shui¹.

7 Duty must be paid on goods.

8 係稅關收稅嘅. Hai₃ shui³ kwaan¹ shau¹ shui³ ke⁵.

8 The customs house receives the duty.

9 國有國法, 家有家法.
Kwok₀ yau₂ kwok₀ faat₀ ka¹ yau₂ ka¹ faat₀.

9 Nations have their laws and families their rules.

10 香港嘅例唔俾人帶酒入口.
Heung¹ kong² ke⁵ lai₃ m₁ pei² yan₁ taai³ tsau² yap₄ hau².

10 Hongkong ordinances prohibit people from bringing wine into the port.

The Fifty-eighth Exercise—(On the Senate and the Customs.)

1 Is this the Senate House ?
    Ni^1 kaan^1 hai$_3$ kwok$_0$ *ui$_3$ m$_1$ hai$_3$?
    呢 間 係 國 會 唔 係.

2 Yes, that house is the Senate (Council Chamber).
    Hai,. koh^2 kaan^1 hai$_3$ kwok$_0$ *ui$_3$
    係, 个 間 係 國 會.

3 Is the Senate the same as the Customs House ?
    Kwok$_0$ *ui$_3$ t'ung$_1$ shui^3 kwaan^1 m$_1$ t'ung$_1$ ni^1 ?
    國 會 同 稅 關 唔 同 呢.

4 No, the Senate is not the same as the Customs House.
    M$_1$ t'ung$_1$, kwok$_0$ *ooi$_3$ m$_1$ t'ung$_1$ shui^3 kwaan^1
    唔 同, 國 會 唔 同 稅 關.

5 What is the difference between these two ?
    Kwok$_0$ *ui$_3$ t'ung$_1$ shui^3 kwaan^1 yau$_2$ mat^4 fan^1 pit$_4$ ni^1?
    國 會 同 稅 關 有 乜 分 別 呢.

6 The Senate attends to the affairs of the country, the customs attends to the duties (on goods).
    Kwok$_0$ *ui$_3$ hai$_3$ ta^2 lei$_2$ kwok$_0$ ka^1 ke^3 s$_7_3$, shui^3
    kwaan^1 hai$_3$ ta^2 lei$_2$ shau^1 shui^3
    國會係打理國家嘅事, 稅關係打理收稅.

7 Citizens should pay the duty, why do some people avoid paying (smuggle).
    Tso$_3$ kwok$_0$ man$_1$ ying^1 tong^1 naap$_4$ shui^3, tim^2 kaai^2
    yau$_2$ ti^1 yan$_1$ tsau^2 shui^3 ni^1 ?
    做國民應當納稅, 點解有的人走稅呢?

8 Those who smuggle, are not in accordance with the laws.
    Tsau^2 shui^3 koh^3 ti^1 yan$_1$ hai$_3$ m$_1$ hop$_4$ faat$_0$ ke^3
    走 稅 个 的 人, 係 唔 合 法 嘅.

9 Has Hongkong an ordinance forbidding bringing wine in.?
    Heung^1 kong^2 yau$_2$ ting$_3$ lai$_3$, m$_1$ pei^2 taai^3 tsau^2 yap$_4$
    hau^2 mo$_2$ ni^1? 香港有定例, 唔俾帶酒入口冇呢.

10 Yes, tobacco also may not be brought in, if duty is paid it may be.
    Yau$_2$, in^1 to^1 m$_1$ pei^2 taai^3 yap$_4$ hau^2, naap$_4$ shui^3
    tsau$_3$ tak^4 有, 煙都唔俾帶入口, 納稅就得.

THE FIFTY-NINTH LESSON

第 五 十 九 課—Tai₃ ng₂ shap₄ kaau² foh³

1	商	Sheung¹—Commerce, merchant	6	已	I₂—Already	
2	務	Mo₃—Affairs, activities	7	紀	Kei²— Arrange, record, a broker	
3	淡	Taam₃ (T'aam₂)— Insipid, weak	8	承	Shing₁—Receive orders, undertake, contain	
4	旺	Wong₃—Flourishing	9	辦	Paan₃—To manage, prepare, transact	
5	經	King¹—Already, past tense, a classic, the warp	10	妥	T'oh₂—Safe, arrange, ready	

1 做生意人係商家. Tso₃ shaang¹ i¹ yan₁ hai₃ sheung¹ ka¹

People who do business are merchants.

2 商家嘅事係商務. Sheung¹ ka¹ ke³ sz₃ hai₃ sheung¹ mo₃.

The affairs of merchants are trade (or commerce).

3 近日香港商務好淡. Kan₃ yat₄ heung⁴ kong² sheung¹ mo₃ ho² taam₃.

Business is very weak (slack) in Hongkong lately.

4 人人想的商務旺番. Yan₁ yan₁ seung² ti¹ sheung¹ mo₃ wong₃ faan¹

Everyone hopes that business may prosper again.

5 但係要經過好耐時候至旺得番 Taan₂ hai₃ iu³ king¹ kwoh³ ho² noi₃ shi₁ hau₃ chi³ wong₃ tak⁴ faan¹.

But it will be a long time before it is prosperous again.

6 佢已經做完佢嘅工. K'ui₂ i₂ king¹ tso₃ uen₁ k'ui₂ ke³ kung¹.

He has already finished his work.

7 經紀同人賣貨要聽佣. King¹ kei² t'ung₁ yan₁ maai₃ foh³ iu⁵ chaan₃ yung².

Brokers selling goods for people make commission.

8 有一間行招人承接一單工程. Yau₂ yat⁴ kaan¹ hong₁ chiu¹ yan₁ shing₁ tsip₀ yat⁴ taan¹ kung¹ ch'ing₁.

There is a firm calling for tenders for a piece of work.

9 有人同人做承辦人. Yau₂ yan₁ t'ung₁ yan₁ tso₃ shing₁ paan₃ yan₁.

Some people undertake to act as executors for others.

10 呢个買辦好妥當嘅. Ni¹ koh³ maai₂ paan₃ ho² t'oh₂ tong³ ke³.

This compradore is very satisfactory (safe).

The Fifty-ninth Exercise—(On Losses in Business.)

1 Formerly a merchant, opened a shop.

Kau₁ shi₁ yau₂ yat⁴ koh³ sheung¹ yan₁ hoi¹. yat⁴ kaan¹ p'o³ *t'au₁ 舊時有一个商人，開一間舖頭．

2 to deal in foreign goods. At first it was fairly prosperous, afterwards the landlord wanted the shop.

Tso₁ maai₂ maai₃ yeung₁ foh³ ke˙ shaang¹ i⁵; hei² ch'oh¹ kei² wong₃, hau₃ loi₁ uk⁴ chue² iu³ faan¹ p'o³ 做買賣洋貨嘅生意，起初幾旺，後來屋主要番舖

3 He went to talk matters over with the landlord. The landlord said he must raise the rent.

K'ui₂ hui¹ t'ung₁ uk⁴ chue² kong² sho³, uk⁴ chue² wa₃ iu³ hei² tso¹ 佢去同屋主講數，屋主話要起租．

4 because lately rates are high; seeing that it was very difficult to remove his shop.

Yan¹ wai₃ kan₃ loi₁ tei₃ shui³ kwai³, k'ui₂ t'ai² kin³ poon¹ p'o³. hai₁ yat⁴ kin₁ kik₄ naan₁ ke˙ sz₃ 因為近來地稅貴。佢睇見撤舖，係一件極難嘅事

5 he must have a suitable place, so he agreed with the landlord.

M₁ hop₄ tei₃ wai₃ m₁ tak⁴, shoh² i₂ k'ui₂ ying¹ shing₁ uk⁴ chue² 唔合地位，唔得，所以佢應承屋主．

6 After a short time, all business fell off and the brokers seeing business so poor.

Mo₂ kei² *noi₁ kok₀ hong₁ shaang¹ i³ to¹ taam₃, koh² ti¹ king¹ kei² kin³ shaang¹ i³ taam₃. vap₄ sik⁴ shiu² 冇幾耐各行生意都淡，个的輕紀見生意淡．入息少

7 and their income so little, cheated him, his business was constantly losing money, and he wanted to get someone to take it over, no one was willing to carry it on.

Shoh² i₂ ngaak⁴ k'ui₂, k'ui₂ ke³ shaang¹ i³ yat⁴ lo₃ shit₄ poon², seung² wan² yan₁ ting² shau², mo₂ yan₁ hang² shing₁ paan₃ 所以呃佢，佢嘅生意一路貼本，想攞人頂手，冇人肯承辦

8 He said to people, it is really very hard to do business, you put in capital, expend your energy, and yet lose, it is very disastrous.

K'ui₂ tui³ yan₁ kong², tso₃ shaang¹ i³ chan¹ hai₃ ho² naan₁, lok₄ poon² ts'in₁, yung₃ tsing¹ shan₁, chung₁ iu³ shit₄ poon², shap₄ fan¹ m₁ t'oh₂ lok₀ 佢對人講，做生意興係好難，落本錢，用精神，重要貼本，十分唔安略．

第六十課—Tai₃ luk₄ shap₄ foh³

1	賊	ᵗTs'aak₄—*Robber, thief.*		
2	搶	Ts'eung²—*Steal, snatch.*		
3	偷	T'au¹—*Steal.*		
4	差	Ch'aai¹—*Police.*		
5	拉	Laai¹—*Arrest.*		
6	罪	Tsui₃—*Sin, Offence.*		
7	審	Sham²—*Try a case.*		
8	官	Kun¹—*Official.*		
9	監	Kaam¹—*Prison, oversee.*		
10	兵	Ping¹—*Soldiers.*		

1 佢係賊唔係小手.
K'ui₂ hai₃ ts'aak₄ m₁ hai₃ siu² shau²

1 He is a robber not a petty thief.

2 佢搶你乜野.
k'ui₂ ts'eung² nei₂ mat⁴ ye₂?

2 What did he steal of yours?

3 唔係搶我野, 佢去我屋踭偷野.
M₁ hai₃ ts'eung² ngoh₂ ve₂, k'ui₂ hui³ ngoh₂ uk⁴ k'ei² t'au¹ ye₂

3 He did not snatch my things, he went to my house and stole things.

4 差人點知佢偷野呢.
Ch'aai¹ yan₁ tim² chi¹ k'ui₂ t'au¹ ye₂ ni¹?

4 How did the police know that he stole things.

5 我聽開佢入屋, 後來我叫差人去拉佢.
Ngoh₂ t'eng¹ man₁ k'ui₂ yap₄ uk⁴, hau₂ loi₁ ngoh₂ kiu³ ch'aai¹ yan₁ hui³ laai₁ k'ui₂

5 I heard him come into the house and afterwards called the police to arrest him.

6 你中意定佢有罪唔呢.
Nei₂ chung¹ i³ teng₃ k'ui₂ yau₂ tsui₃ m₁ ni¹?

6 Do you want to determine his offence.

7 我不能定佢有罪, 要審過然後可以定罪.
Ngoh₂ pat⁴ nang₁ teng₃ k'ui₂ yau₂ tsui₃, iu³ sham² kwoh³ in₁ hau₂, hoh² i, teng₃ tsui₃

7 I cannot fix his offence, he must be tried before he is convicted.

8 官巳經審過話佢有罪.
Kun¹ i₂ king¹ sham² kwoh³ wa₃ k'ui₂ yau₂ tsui₃

8 The magistrate has tried him and convicted him.

9 有罪要坐監, 有罪就放人
Yau₂ tsui₃ iu³ ts'oh₂ kaam¹, mo₂ tsui₃ tsau₂ fong³ yan₁

9 If he is convicted he must go to prison, if he is innocent he will be released.

10 做兵去偷野, 真係笑話咯
Tso₂ ping¹ hui³ t'au¹ ye₂, chan¹ hai₃ siu³ wa₃ lok₀

10 A soldier stealing things this is funny.

The Sixtieth Exercise—(A Thief.)

1 Yesterday he came to visit me, I invited him to dinner.

Tsok₄ yat₄ k'ui₂ lai₁ t'aam³ ngoh₂, ngoh₂ ts'ing² k'ui₂ shik₄ ts'aan¹ 昨日佢嚟探我，我請佢食餐.

2 I told him a certain matter, a few days ago, at his friend's house robbers went in and stole some things.

Ngoh₂ kong² yat⁴ kin₃ sz₃ k'ui₂ t'ing¹, k'ui₂ ke° p'ang₁ yau₂ uk⁴ k'ei², sin¹ kei² yat₄ pei² ts'aak₄ yap₄ uk⁴ t'au¹ ye₂

我講一件事佢聽，佢嘅朋友屋踪. 先幾日俾賊入屋偷野

3 At first no one knew, afterwards he heard a sound (noise), and called out "thief" in a loud voice, Hearing h'm call, the thieves ran in different directions.

Sin' shi₁ mo₂ yan₁ chi¹, tsoi₃ hau₃ t'eng¹ man₁ vau₂ sheng¹, k'ui₂ tsau₃ taai₃ sheng¹ kiu' ts'aak₄ a³, ti² ts'aak₄ t'eng¹ man₁ k'ui₂ kiu°, kok₀ vau₂ kok₀ tsau²

先時冇人知，在後聽聞有聲，佢就大聲叫賊呀，的賊聽聞佢叫，各有各走.

4 But one could not get away, he ran and shut the door, and the thief could not escape, so they blew a police whistle and shortly a policeman came and took the thief off to the police station.

Taan₃ hai₃ yau₂ yat⁴ koh³ ts'aak₄ tsau² m₁ hei², k'ui₂ tsau₃ hui³ shaan¹ moon₁, koh° ts'aak₄ mo₂ faat₀ hoh² i₂ tsau₃, kom² k'ui₂ tei₃ tsau₃ ch'ui¹ ngan₁ kai¹, mo₂ kei² *noi₃ yau₂ ch'aai¹ yan₁ to' tseung¹ koh³ ts'aak₄ laai¹ hui³ ch'aai¹ koon²

但係有一个賊走唔起，佢就去閂門，个賊冇法可以走，叫佢哋就吹銀雞，冇幾耐有差人到，將个賊拉去差館.

5 Next day the case was tried, the thief would not confess, the magistrate asked him, why he was a thief, he said, he had no tool to eat, he asked why do you not work, he said, he could not find work, the official seeing that he was not old, and went into houses to steal, condemned him to six months imprisonment.

Tai₃ i₃ yat⁴ hoi¹ t'ong₁ sham², koh° ts'aak₄ m₁ ving₃ yau₂ tsui₃, kun¹ man₁ k'ui₂ tim² kaai² iu³ tso₃ ts'aak₄, k'ui₂ taap₀ wa₃ mo₂ faan₃ shik₄, kun¹ tsoi³ man₃ k'ui₂ tim² kaai² m₁ tso₃ kung¹, k'ui₂ taap₀ wan² kung¹ m₁ to², kun¹ kin³ k'ui₂ nin₁ kei² m₁ hai, lo₂, hui³ tso₃ ts'aak₄ yap₄ uk⁴ t'au¹ ye₂, teng₃ k'ui₂ yau₂ tsui₃, iu³ ts'oh₀ luk₄ koh² net₄ kaam¹.

第二日開堂審，个賊唔認有罪，官問佢點解要做賊，佢答話冇飯食，官再問佢點解唔做工，佢答搵工唔倒，官見佢年紀唔係老，去做賊入屋偷野，定佢有罪，要坐六个月監

書名：英粵通語Cantonese for everyone——香港大學粵語教材（一九三一）
系列：心一堂　香港・澳門雙城成長系列
原著：H. R. Wells 編著
主編・責任編輯：陳劍聰

出版：心一堂有限公司
通訊地址：香港九龍旺角彌敦道六一〇號荷李活商業中心十八樓〇五—〇六室
深港讀者服務中心：中國深圳市羅湖區立新路六號羅湖商業大廈負一層〇〇八室
電話號碼：(852) 9027-7110
網址：publish.sunyata.cc
淘宝店地址：https://sunyata.taobao.com
微店地址：　https://weidian.com/s/1212826297
臉書：　　　https://www.facebook.com/sunyatabook
讀者論壇：　http://bbs.sunyata.cc

香港發行：香港聯合書刊物流有限公司
地址：香港新界荃灣德士古道220～248號荃灣工業中心16樓
電話號碼：(852) 2150-2100
傳真號碼：(852) 2407-3062
電郵：info@suplogistics.com.hk
網址：http://www.suplogistics.com.hk

台灣發行：秀威資訊科技股份有限公司
地址：台灣台北市內湖區瑞光路七十六巷六十五號一樓
電話號碼：+886-2-2796-3638
傳真號碼：+886-2-2796-1377
網絡書店：www.bodbooks.com.tw
心一堂台灣秀威書店讀者服務中心：
地址：台灣台北市中山區松江路二〇九號1樓
電話號碼：+886-2-2518-0207
傳真號碼：+886-2-2518-0778
網址：http://www.govbooks.com.tw

中國大陸發行　零售：深圳心一堂文化傳播有限公司
深圳地址：深圳市羅湖區立新路六號羅湖商業大廈負一層008室
電話號碼：(86)0755-82224934

版次：二零二一年三月初版，平裝

心一堂微店二維碼　　心一堂淘寶店二維碼

定價：　港幣　　　九十八元正
　　　　新台幣　　四百五十元正

國際書號 ISBN 978-988-8583-72-0